Acknowledgments

This book is for all my wonderful friends on Twitter, who encouraged me to continue when writing was tough. You laughed at my coffee/yogurt exploits and assured me that I'm really not the worst writer in the world (probably).

I couldn't have finished the book without your help.

Thanks so much.

Books by SM Reine

SEASONS OF THE MOON SERIES
Six Moon Summer
All Hallows' Moon
Long Night Moon
Gray Moon Rising

THE DESCENT SERIES
Death's Hand
The Darkest Gate
Damnation Marked

For Jude
Always.

Prelude

The Cage

The werewolf should have dominated the night, but humans had taken charge with guns and silver. The beast was cut off from the moon by iron bars and helpless to fight. Few human things made sense to her primitive mind, but one thing stood out above everything else: She had been caged.

The wolf thrashed, shrieking when her flesh touched upon silver-laced iron. She tried to jerk away, but there was nowhere safe to flee. The hunters had placed her upon a bed of wolfsbane.

A pair of legs moved into view, and the wolf smelled the familiar odor of leather. It would have been comforting if he hadn't been aiming a rifle at her face. She whined.

"Do it already, Seth," snapped a woman. "I will if you won't." The wolf's strength waned, and she flung herself at the cage one last time. Her flesh sizzled. She collapsed.

The rifle swayed as Seth knelt beside her.

"Shoot it!"

"I'm sorry, Rylie," he whispered.

And then he squeezed the trigger.

One

Homecoming

When the sun sank beneath the hills, the trucker turned on his headlights to illuminate the road. Night fell quickly in the middle of nowhere. There weren't any streetlights for miles, much less city, so he knew it would be black in minutes.

His passenger bounced her knee and drummed her knuckles against the window. She was fixated by the passing landscape even though there was nothing to look at but long grass and the occasional tree. Her blond hair was pulled into a messy bun and her fingernails were chewed so short that her thumb bled.

The trucker watched her from the corner of his eye. She was starting to tremble.

"You okay?" he asked.

She nodded a little too quickly. "Yeah. Sure. I'm fine. Is this as fast as we can go?"

He chuckled. "I'm in a hurry too, sweetheart, but I've gotta go the speed limit. Another speeding ticket could make me lose my job."

"Going slow could make you lose more than that," she muttered.

"What did you say?"

"Nothing."

A rabbit bounced past the headlights, and her head whipped around so she could stare at the place it vanished. There was something unnatural about the way she moved. It was like everything startled her. The trucker wondered if she was on cocaine or meth or something else. Nobody acted like that unless they had taken drugs—or if they were nuts.

He suspected there was something wrong with his mysterious passenger when he picked her up at a truck stop two states back. How many cute teenage girls hitchhiked on semis? Just prostitutes. But this kid was no hooker, and the trucker wouldn't have done anything if she was. He had a son her age back home. His picture was taped to the dashboard.

The girl seemed pretty normal for the first few hours— quiet, but normal—but she got more nervous as time went on. Now her skin was flushed and her pupils were too wide.

"You ever going to tell me your name?" he asked. It was the first time he'd tried to talk with her since Colorado.

"Rylie. My name's Rylie." She raked her fingernails up and down her shoulder, leaving red tracks on tan skin.

"Pretty name. I've got a niece named Kiley. She's in the chess club at school, and..." He trailed off as she shuddered, hugging her backpack against her body. "You okay?"

"Moon's coming soon."

"Yeah?" He leaned forward to look at the sky. All the trucker could see were clouds. "How can you tell? Won't there be a new moon tonight?"

"I'm in a hurry. There aren't going to be any cops out here. Can't you...?"

"Relax," he said. "We'll get there when we get there." He watched her from the corner of his eye. "How old are you? Sixteen? Seventeen?" She didn't respond. "Drugs seemed like the cool thing to do when I was your age, but they ruined my life. I lost my family and spent years in rehab. Addiction is brutal."

Rylie looked startled. "I'm not addicted to drugs."

"I didn't think I was addicted either, but—"

"No, I mean, I'm not taking anything. Okay?"

"Okay, okay. You're not addicted. Then what are you running from?" he asked.

"Nothing. I'm going to live with my aunt. She moved out here from Colorado a couple of months ago, so I'm going to work on her new ranch."

"And your aunt lets you hitchhike?"

She lifted her chin stubbornly. "Nobody *lets* me do anything anymore."

"Uh huh."

She wasn't going to talk to him about her problems. No big deal. The trucker remembered being in her place years ago. He hadn't wanted to talk about it all that much, either. Getting past his denial was the first step to recovery.

They drove on in silence, and she kept scratching herself. Probably meth. It looked like meth.

Even though he knew he couldn't help her until she was ready to help herself, he had to try. "I could drop you off at a hospital if you want," he suggested.

"I'm not going to a hospital!" she snarled. Her eyes flashed a reflective gold, like an animal.

"Holy mother of—"

Rylie looked out the window again, cutting him off with a slam of her knuckles against the glass. "My friend Tyler says speed limits are suggestions." She had calmed down and sounded normal. Not growling. Not like...

He was imagining things.

He patted his pocket in search of caffeine pills. The trucker hadn't slept in over a day, and now he was hallucinating. But his pockets were empty. "Maybe I'll go a little faster," he muttered. He'd get the kid to her aunt and pull over to catch some sleep.

The trucker rolled down his window, letting the cold air slap him in the face. When the clouds parted, there was no moon. It was a dark night.

Rylie groaned and doubled over.

"Hey there," he said. "You okay?"

Her fingernails dug into her sides. "I'm—ugh—I'm *fine*." Rylie shoved her backpack to the floor of the truck and pressed her forehead to her knees.

She arched her spine. It ridged under her t-shirt like it could tear the fabric.

"You don't look fine."

"I need out. Stop the truck!"

"What? But—" A sign whizzed by, indicating that the next town wasn't for fifteen miles. "There's nothing out here. I can't drop you off; you'd get eaten by—"

She lifted her head and slammed it down again. Something made a popping sound, and it reminded the trucker of the time he caught his arm on a passing trailer and wrenched his shoulder from the socket.

Rylie snapped her head to the side. Her bleeding gums stained her teeth and the skin around her nose was stretching—her nose was breaking—

"Jesus Christ!"

"Stop the truck," she growled. "*Now*."

He swerved and tried to press himself against his door to get away from this *thing—it wasn't a teenage girl, not anymore*, her blond hair was falling out in huge clumps on the seat—but the huge cab of the truck was suddenly too small.

She threw her head back as she screamed and dug her nails into his dashboard. They weren't fingernails anymore.

He threw the brake even though they weren't on the shoulder of the road. They weren't even on the correct side, for that matter. He didn't care.

Something snapped and cracked. Rylie's jaw unhinged and slid forward. She spit blood onto her jeans.

The trucker's hand fumbled for the door. Locked.

"Oh no—oh *God*—"

She flung herself against the dashboard, and then arched in the other direction, straining her feet and head back like a bow. Something was wrong with her knees.

Yeah, but what isn't wrong with this thing?

"Get out!" she shrieked, and flecks of bloody spit slapped against his face.

Rylie lunged for him, claws flashing.

His finger caught the lock. The door fell open.

He fell onto the pavement and slammed the door behind him. The trucker couldn't think straight, because every time he tried to broach the idea that some poor hitchhiking kid had turned into *something*—something not human—he felt a level of panic very close to insanity.

The cab rocked back and forth. He couldn't see what was inside from this angle, but he could hear shrieking and howling. Those noises couldn't come from a human mouth.

Because she's not human.

"Oh Jesus Christ," he said.

Fear wheeled through his skull. Management would have everything from the neck up if they found out he abandoned his truck. And the goods, the electronics he was supposed to be getting to that warehouse—

Something slammed into the windshield. The safety glass spiderwebbed.

Forget management.

The trucker ran as fast as he could, rolling his tubby body along at a speed he hadn't managed since he was two hundred pounds lighter and twenty years younger.

Howls followed him into the night.

• ○ •

Rylie awoke to a cool breeze playing across her skin and a feeling of dread.

Oh no. Not again.

She opened her eyes. A tiny black bug crawled along the grass by her head, and a thin layer of mist hovered over the ground. Her skin felt soggy.

Shutting her eyes, Rylie tried to force memories of the previous evening to emerge. As usual, she couldn't remember what happened after she... changed. But she remembered a trucker. Nice guy. Smelled like gas station bathrooms and tobacco, but nice.

Her mouth was sticky, and there was a warm, sated feeling in her stomach that she recognized. It was the same way she had felt after killing a deer over the summer.

She wiped a hand over her mouth, and her fingers came away bloody.

Was the trucker... alive?

Rylie sat up, scrubbing a hand over her chin to clean it. The damp grass made her shiver. Ants marched along her knee.

She lifted her head and sniffed. The smells of the pasture splashed through her mind: meat and blood, soil and grass, honey in the comb, and a musky, chemical scent meant to mimic flowers. It was her own smell. She had picked the weirdest perfume she could find at the drug store so it would be easy to track.

Trailing the perfume down the hill, she found shreds of cloth tangled in the barbed wire fence. She suddenly recalled agonizing pain scraping down her back as her fur stuck on something—but it was gone as soon as it came. She never remembered her time as a wolf once she turned back.

Rylie picked the remains of her clothes out of the wire. There were more holes than cloth in her t-shirt, and the seams had burst when she changed, too. But it covered the important parts. It was better than nothing.

SM Reine

Her jeans were a little further down the hill, and in even worse condition. Rylie had to hold them over her hips as she plodded toward the road. She had no idea how to explain this to her aunt. She needed to buy new clothes before showing up at her door.

She stopped at the bottom of the hill. There were lumps all over the pasture in front of her, but it was too dark to make out any detail. Rylie approached the closest one with fear twisting in her stomach.

It was—or at least, it used to be—a cow. But the only way Rylie could tell was because of its distinctive odor, like manure and hay. The thing on the ground didn't look much like a cow. Neither did the other three carcasses, either. She had a feeling she knew what had happened.

"Oh no," she whispered.

Something clicked twice, *chick-chuck.* Rylie had seen enough action movies to know the sound of a shotgun being pumped.

"Hands up. Turn around. Slowly now—nothing sudden."

Rylie obeyed. Her heart skipped a beat.

It wasn't the first time she'd been at gunpoint, but it was just as scary this time as it had been the last time, so it took her a moment to realize who was aiming at her. A gray-haired woman with hard lines framing her mouth braced the butt of the shotgun against her shoulder, and a cowboy hat hung down her back by a bolero tie.

"Aunt Gwyneth?" she gasped.

The shotgun dropped. "*Rylie?*"

Two

The Suspect

"I'd say you've got a lot of explaining to do, but I hate to state the obvious."

Aunt Gwyneth sat on the edge of the kitchen table with her shotgun leaning against the counter. Rylie cupped a mug of coffee between her hands. She didn't like coffee, but it was all her aunt had to drink other than dirty well water, and she desperately wanted the heat.

She pulled her feet under her on the chair and wrapped the blanket around her legs like a protective shield. She was wearing sweat pants and a shirt borrowed from her aunt, but she still felt exposed.

I got bitten by a werewolf at summer camp and now I'm a monster that goes into murderous rages on every new and full moon. How are you doing, Aunt Gwyn?

Somehow, she didn't think that would go over well.

"Coyotes," Rylie said.

Gwyn raised an eyebrow. "Coyotes?"

"They attacked the cows." Her voice was tiny.

"Coyotes are cowards, honey. They eat rabbits and house cats. They don't go after the herd."

Rylie smiled feebly. "Crazy rabid coyotes?"

Her aunt's eyes narrowed. "I might buy an animal going nuts and killing my cows, but that doesn't explain how you ended up in my field this morning with your clothes shredded. What the heck is going on? You told me you had a ride here."

"I did. I caught a ride with Frank."

"Frank?"

"He drives a semi," Rylie said.

"*What?*" It looked like Gwyn was in pain. "Let me get this straight. You told me you had a ride here, but you hitchhiked instead? Babe, you could have been seriously hurt. You could have been *killed*. Is this 'Frank' why your clothes are torn?"

"No! No, Aunt Gwyn, it wasn't like that at all. He was really nice."

"Then what happened?"

Rylie braced herself for the lie. She sucked at lying. "He let me off on your road. I thought I'd get in earlier, but I ended up walking late last night. I saw some coyotes go after the cows. They came after me too, but I jumped through the fence and escaped. I fell down the hill, though. That's why everything is torn."

"And then you went back to look at the cows," Gwyn said.

"I was lost."

"So you're telling me you didn't bring anything with you? Not even another outfit?"

She took a sip of coffee to give herself time to think. "I forgot my backpack in Frank's truck."

Her aunt pinched the bridge of her nose. "You can tell me the truth, Rylie. I know you didn't kill my cows—I saw the wounds. It was some kind of animal. So whatever you did that you're not telling me, I'm not going to get mad at you."

"That *is* the truth," she said.

"It's a pretty tall tale you expect me to believe." Gwyn shook her head. "Are you okay?"

Okay? No. Definitely not okay. "I'm not injured."

"I guess that's something." She refilled Rylie's empty coffee mug. "I thought Jessica was going to bring you out here."

"My mom's been busy since I let her take over dad's business." The mention of Rylie's dead father—her aunt's brother—was enough to kill the conversation.

"All right. Follow me."

Gwyn led her from the kitchen. The ranch house was small. There was no formal dining room, and the three bedrooms were lined up on one side with a single bathroom. It was much more modest than her aunt's last place, which had always been filled with workers and friends. Everything here was lonely and quiet. Rylie wondered what changed, but was too afraid to ask.

They went to the second bedroom on the left. Gwyn's room was at the end—Rylie could tell by the bed covered in silky red sheets. Her night stand was covered in orange pill bottles.

She shut her door. "That one's mine. This one's yours."

Rylie's bedroom was a white box with wood floors and a bay window. It looked like it used to be wallpapered, but it had since been torn down, leaving glue stains. An old corkboard was hung on one wall.

"I haven't dragged the dresser in from the garage. That's your job," Gwyn said. "You can do whatever you want in here: new paint, new carpet, furniture, whatever. Anything short of setting it on fire. I'll go into the town hardware store to get paint for the kitchen tomorrow after school, so maybe you'll want some too?"

"School?" Rylie asked, startled.

"Yes, school. What did you expect?"

"I thought I was coming here to help around the ranch."

Her aunt grinned, and it wasn't a pleasant expression at all. "You're fifteen. You can't become jaded and give up on society until you're at least seventeen. Jessica helped me enroll you at the high school in town."

Her heart dropped. "But..."

"You can paint lime polka dots on the walls of my house, but you can't sit around all day. You're going to school tomorrow. Got it?"

She kicked the door frame. "Okay. Fine. Can I have a minute alone?"

"You going to kill more of my cows if I turn my back on you?" Gwyn asked. Rylie's jaw dropped. "I'm kidding, girl. Don't be such an easy mark. I'll be picking fruit in the orchard if you want to find me."

She left. Rylie sank to the bed and buried her face in her hands. The empty room felt like it was crowding in around her.

Nothing had been the same since camp. After her first real change, Rylie had woken up to find herself naked in the forest with no company but the squirrels, who weren't too keen on having her around, either. It wasn't until a park ranger found her and dragged her back to civilization that Rylie learned she had lost two full weeks of her life.

She still didn't know what happened during that time. Rylie suspected she must have transformed again since the moon was waning when the ranger found her. She wasn't sure if she had become human again between the moons or if she had been a wolf for weeks.

They declared her healthy but dehydrated at the town hospital, where Jessica picked her up. The city was even worse after her change. Rylie barely tolerated three days in her mom's condo before calling Aunt Gwyneth.

She had been sure she could make it to the ranch before changing again, even if she hitchhiked. But obviously she hadn't.

Rylie remembered riding with the trucker. She also remembered waking up with the cows.

But between that... nothing.

Was this her life now? A series of moments between blackouts? Rylie had floated through the last month in a dreamlike haze. The entire summer felt like a nightmare. Her dad's death, almost getting mugged, Jericho and Cassidy's attack on the camp, Seth...

No, not Seth. He could never be a nightmare.

The last time she remembered seeing him, he had been dragged off by the werewolf who changed her. When she woke up in the forest two weeks later, all traces of him were gone. She still didn't know if he was dead or not.

Rylie studied the corkboard. It must have been left by the previous owners, since her aunt wasn't an artist and several pencil sketches had been pinned to its surface. They illustrated the house and the fields around it, including stables and a little pond. Boring. Safe. Ordinary. Three qualities Rylie's life would never again possess.

She ripped down the pictures and stuffed them under the bed.

• ◯ •

One minute, Rylie drifted in a dreamless haze, caught in the confusing place between asleep and awake. The next minute, her bedroom door slammed open and her room was flooded in light.

She almost fell onto the floor. Rylie had her hackles up until she recognized her aunt's silhouette. "Get out of bed!" Gwyn ordered, jerking the sheets off her bed.

Swallowing a growl, Rylie glanced at her fingers—which were tipped with fingernails, not claws—and she squinted through the light at her aunt. She was already in Carhartts, work boots, and a sweater.

"What time is it?"

"It's time to do chores. Why aren't you getting dressed? I told you to get up!"

The sun wasn't even coming through the windows yet. Rylie rubbed the sleep from her eyes. "I thought I was going to school today."

That cruel grin winked at the corner of Gwyn's mouth. "You are."

"Uh," Rylie said. She couldn't think of a better response.

Aunt Gwyn left her to dress, but she returned after about fifteen seconds. Rylie pulled a borrowed pair of jeans over her hips and tried to get the belt tight enough to keep them above her underwear. Her aunt was muscular and much bulkier than she was.

Gwyn carried a huge bag of feed over her shoulder, and she looked annoyed to see her niece half-dressed. "You might want a shirt before we start working."

"I'm not done getting dressed!"

"Too bad. Move it!"

She pulled a sweater over her head as she stumbled out the back door. Static made Rylie's hair stick straight up. Even with a heavy bag of feed over her shoulder, Aunt Gwyn's stride was twice as long as hers, and she swept through the garden toward the chicken coop. The sky was black and the soil was sodden with dew.

Stuffing her foot into one oversized boot, then the next, she tried not to trip over the laces as Gwyn shoved the bag into her arms. Rylie threw it over her shoulder. Her aunt gave her a funny look, and Rylie suddenly remembered that she was supposed to be a normal teenage girl instead of a super-strong werewolf. She feigned weakness. "Oof," she said, staggering.

It might have been the worst performance of her life, but it was good enough for Gwyn. "Feed the chickens, collect the eggs, and meet me in the barn."

Rylie hesitated. Animals didn't like her anymore. The last time she had run across horses, her collarbone had been broken. They were a lot bigger than chickens, but... "I don't think that's a good idea."

Gwyn was already gone.

Standing back amongst the cabbages placed her upwind of the chickens so they wouldn't notice her. The bag of feed felt like an oversized pillow to her, but the lead weight of worry in her gut anchored her to the spot.

So what if the chickens didn't like her? What could they do?

"Feed the chickens," Rylie muttered. "Collect the eggs." A rooster cried out mockingly on top of the coop.

She eased inside the gate. It smelled like the henhouse hadn't been cleaned in a couple of days, and there were flies everywhere, but the hens weren't making noise. Maybe they were still asleep. Maybe she could get in and out before they even—

Feathers exploded around her. The rooster panicked and cackled, flapping its wings to send droppings flying everywhere. The hens awoke all at once, gabbling and bursting out of the coop.

Shocked, Rylie dropped the bag of feed. It opened and dumped across the ground. "Oh no!"

The presence of food didn't calm the chickens. The wire enclosure rattled as the rooster flew at her, trying to *attack* her, and it was so ridiculous that she would have laughed if it wasn't also a little terrifying. And if her stomach wasn't growling.

Rylie imagine snapping her jaws on the neck of a hen and shaking it until its spine snapped. She thought how good it would taste, even if it was a little small, and...

Wiping drool off her chin, she backtracked out of the coop and latched the gate behind her. *Gross.* Rylie's stomach turned. The chickens smelled awful, not delicious. Those were *not* good thoughts to have.

Her aunt was saddling up a horse when Rylie poked her head around the barn door. "Where are the eggs? And where's the rest of the feed?" Gwyn asked.

"There weren't any eggs."

"And...?"

"I dropped the feed bag," Rylie said to her feet.

Her aunt rubbed her face. A deep line had taken up permanent residence between her eyebrows. "Why?"

"It was heavy." When her aunt gave her a Look—the kind of Look that said she was reconsidering having Rylie help around the ranch—she hurried to add, "I'm *really* sorry."

"You know what? It's fine. Come in here and saddle up Butch. You're going to ride out to the goat pasture with me, and then we'll check on the cows."

Rylie stared at Butch without coming into the barn. He looked about a million years old and as gentle as a bunny on Vicodin.

"I can't," she whispered.

"What's that? Speak up."

"I can't ride horses anymore. I'm... uh, I'm scared of them."

Gwyn planted her hands on her hips. "Stop talking nonsense. You've ridden my horses since you could barely reach their knees. I don't have time for games, so get in here and saddle up."

"Isn't there something else I could do? Something that doesn't involve animals?"

"Honey, this is a ranch. *Everything* is for the animals. You want me to call Jessica, or are you going to help out?"

Having her mom pick her up sounded almost as fun as getting her collarbone broken by a horse again. Maybe Butch wouldn't notice that she smelled like a wolf. Maybe he'd let her ride him, and she could do her chores... until he realized there was something evil on his back.

"Are you sure there isn't something else I could do?"

Gwyn's eyes narrowed. "I might have something."

And that's how Rylie ended up hauling bales of hay at five thirty in the morning on her first day of school.

It wasn't that bad, actually. Once her aunt stopped watching, she didn't have to pretend the bales were hard to lift, and she was so sleepy that she quickly fell into a zombie-like rhythm. Bend, lift, throw, bend—over and over again.

By the time the sun rose and the ranch hands arrived, Rylie had already unloaded all the hay and arranged it in a neat stack.

Gwyn tipped her hat back with a knuckle to examine Rylie's work. "Well," she said. "All right. Get in the truck. Time for school."

Three

First Day

Her aunt had found a knapsack somewhere and given Rylie a few supplies. She searched through the bag while Gwyn drove the long road into town. There was a notebook, a couple of pens and pencils, and a white binder with a few dividers. She'd also packed a sandwich in the side pouch. It smelled like cheese and avocado.

Rylie's mouth watered, but before she could dig in, her aunt handed her something wrapped in paper. "The one in your bag is for lunch. This is breakfast."

She took a sniff of the paper, and images of sour cream, spinach, beans, and rice came to mind. "What is it?"

"Breakfast burrito. I made it for you last summer, remember?"

"But there's no sausage or eggs," Rylie said.

Gwyn glanced at her. "Aren't you a vegetarian?"

She had been waiting for this question, so she gave her prepared answer: "It was just a phase. I changed my mind over the summer." Actually, Rylie still found the idea of eating animals repulsive, but werewolves didn't do well on a diet of vegetables.

"A phase, huh? Well, if you wake up on time tomorrow, you can eat a real breakfast with me before we start working."

"When is 'on time'?" she asked around a mouthful of tortilla. It tasted like sandpaper to the wolf, but she swallowed it anyway.

"Four."

Not a chance. "Maybe," Rylie said.

The town started to appear bit by bit, like grains of sand scattered across paper. First there were a couple of small farms, and then there was a strip mall that looked like it hadn't been updated since the fifties. Normal houses came next, followed by a gas station, and then Rylie realized they were downtown. It was a wide road with lots of antique stores and a bakery.

She shuddered. A city girl at heart, Rylie had grown up in fear of towns exactly like this one. She used to love hanging out at art galleries, but she got the impression nobody here would have recognized a Monet if they saw one. "Is there a movie theater?"

"Sure, the Valley Cinema. Two screens."

Rylie tried not to start crying.

They turned off at the end of the street and went about a block before stopping. She got out of the truck. The high school buildings were scattered around the lot without any apparent reasoning, and one big tree with yellowing leaves guarded the entrance. Otherwise, it was as barren as the rest of the city—aside from all the teenagers.

They were doing normal teenager things. Milling around to talk, parking their cars, playing hacky sack. It looked like morning at any other high school around the country.

So why was Rylie's heart pounding?

Aunt Gwyneth leaned out the window. "You'll need to get your schedule at the office before you go to class. Think you can handle it?"

No! No, no, no!

"Yeah... I guess."

"Great. See you after school!"

"Gwyn!" Rylie called, trying to make one last effort at summoning her back, but the truck rumbled away without her.

She stared at the high school sign. It loomed in her vision, shaded by the sun at its rear, and Rylie fought not to hyperventilate.

I can't do this. I can't go to high school again.

What if everybody hated her? After her problems at Camp Silver Brook, she couldn't stand the thought of having to meet a whole new group of horrible girls.

Rylie clutched her knapsack like armor, taking deep breaths. She needed the wolf. The wolf wouldn't care about school, nor would it care if nobody liked her. It only cared about the hunger.

Shutting her eyes, she sought out the warm, dark place inside herself where the wolf slept between moons. It hibernated in the days after a change, and it was especially satiated and quiet after getting to eat all those cows. Rylie tried to stir it, but the wolf didn't think high school was worth waking up.

It wouldn't be any help today. She was on her own.

The office was in the first building to the right. A secretary worked on a computer with a huge, blocky monitor that looked like it should have been in a museum. He looked up when she approached, pushing his glasses up his nose.

"Yes?"

"I'm Rylie Gresham. I'm new."

"Oh, Gresham. Right. We're expecting you. Here you go." He handed over her schedule and a copy of the school's map. "Do you need help finding your way around?"

There were four small buildings marked out on the map, and a multipurpose room that served as both cafeteria and gymnasium. Her last high school had wings, the students were known by their ID number, and half of her classes had been in lecture halls.

"I'm fine. Thanks."

"Welcome to our school," he said with a thin smile.

Rylie could feel the weight of the eyes pressing on her as she searched for her classes. Students whispered. Teachers watched her for too long. There were about three hundred people in the entire school, so a new student couldn't have been more obvious unless she blasted a foghorn from the top of the bleachers.

She could hear her name underneath it all, like the whispering of a river: *Rylie.*

Homeroom was supposed to be a half hour period of silent reading. She didn't have a book. The teacher loaned her a dog-eared copy of "The Handmaiden's Tale," but he didn't try to keep everyone quiet, so murmurs rolled through the room. Rylie's sensitive ears heard it all.

I heard she's from the city.

What's she doing here?

She's so skinny.

She looks mean.

Rylie opened her book to a random page and pretended to read, but she couldn't stop listening to everyone. After everything she endured at camp, she felt like she should have been immune to the attention. All she wanted was to be invisible and ignored, and being new in a small farming town was just about the worst way to disappear.

The half hour homeroom period crept along too slowly. When she finally escaped into the fresh air and sunlight, Rylie stood in the quad taking deep breaths with her eyes shut.

When the bell rang for the next period, she opened her eyes to find a short girl standing in front of her.

"What are you doing?" she asked.

"Recharging my solar batteries," Rylie said.

"You're weird."

"Yeah. Thanks."

She moved to find her next class, and the girl followed. "Why did you move here?"

"I was extradited," she said without stopping.

"God, I'm just trying to be friendly. I'm Kathleen, by the way. I'm on the leadership committee. I was going to offer to show you around."

Rylie gave Kathleen a second look. She was one of those girls who had grown *out* rather than *up* when she hit puberty, and she had the unpleasant face of a pig digging through the mud. Even though she didn't look anything like Amber, who taunted Rylie for weeks at camp before getting killed, something about Kathleen brought that horrible girl to mind anyway.

"I know your type," Rylie said in a low voice so nobody else could hear. "Don't mess with me. I will mess you up."

Kathleen looked like she'd been slapped, and she was still standing there when Rylie went into her geography class.

Ms. Reedy hovered over her desk and stared at her through glasses that made her look like an owl. Rylie tried to ignore her, but the teacher didn't move until the bell gave its final chime. Kathleen took her seat just in time.

"Rylie Gresham," Ms. Reedy said.

"What?"

"Would you please come to the front of the class?"

The teacher followed as Rylie went to stand in front of the blackboard and face her classmates. She had spent all morning trying not to look at these people, hoping that they would go away if she ignored them. Now she could do nothing but look at rows of unfamiliar faces.

There was Kathleen, next to a freckled girl who might have been a cheerleader, and then there was a boy with slicked-back brown hair. Only eight in all. Small class.

And they all *stared* at her.

Ms. Reedy's lips twitched in what was either a smile or a grimace. "Tell us about yourself."

I'm a werewolf. I would kill all of you and eat your organs.

"My name is Rylie." She focused on a world map on the back wall. "I'm not from around here."

"What do you like to do?"

Kill.

Her nerves had stirred the werewolf within. It was interested in these young, vulnerable faces. It was thinking about the one exit to the room and how easy it would be to trap everyone inside.

"I like movies and art," Rylie said. *Let me sit down, let me get out of here, I don't want to be up here anymore...*

"And?"

Annoyance clenched in her stomach. Rylie opened her mouth to—to what? Growl? Snap at the teacher? Now *that* would be a great way to start the school year.

She shut her mouth, bit her lip, and sat down at her desk. Her face burned.

Ms. Reedy stared at her. They all did. Kathleen was whispering to someone, and Rylie could feel every word like a nail in the back of her neck. Now that the wolf had awakened, it wasn't happy with such an anticlimax. She tried to ignore it.

After a long, awkward silence, the teacher went to her lectern. "We're going to review chapter four today. Please open your books..."

Rylie.

Her name. Someone was whispering her name.

She dug the fingernails of one hand into her knee while she took the school book from the tray under her desk with the other.

"She snapped at me on the way into class... just trying to be nice..."

Kathleen. It was that girl talking about her, and Rylie remembered how the other girls at camp read her diary. At the time, she had responded by leaving the cabin, but retreating only made her more of a target. She wouldn't be a target anymore. She wasn't prey.

Chapter four. Her eyes blurred. She couldn't make out the page.

"...so weird..."

"...wonder why she would..."

"...what's with her?"

A growl rumbled in her chest. She couldn't stop it.

Kathleen's head was bent over her book, but she was whispering out of the corner of her mouth to someone.

"Stop it!" Rylie hissed.

"What? I wasn't—"

"Just shut up. Shut *up*."

Kathleen's eyes went round. Her lips sealed tight. Her gaze flicked over Rylie's shoulder, and she turned to see Ms. Reedy hovering again.

"Is there a problem?" the teacher asked. The whole class was silent.

"No," she said, her heart pounding. "No problem at all."

They went through the chapter review question by question. Each person had to answer at least one, although Ms. Reedy skipped over Rylie, since she hadn't had the chance to read the book.

Slowly, so slowly, the voices started again.

Rylie... Rylie...

It was that Kathleen girl.

"We're going to get in groups of three to work on the test quiz," Ms. Reedy announced halfway through the class. "You can look up the answers in the book, but no cell phones." She gave a pointed look at Rylie even though her phone didn't get very good reception out in the country.

The teacher separated them into groups, and Rylie ended up with Kathleen and the cheerleader, who turned out to be named Maxine.

SM Reine

"So... do you want to look up different questions, or should we...?" Kathleen ventured. So it was like that, then. She didn't want to work with Rylie. She just wanted to get rid of her. *She was just like Amber.*

"Fine. I'll do it myself," Rylie snapped.

"That's not—"

"Don't pick on me!" She shoved her chair back and flung the book off her desk. Rylie was stronger than ever before. It flipped over and smacked into Kathleen's arm.

"Hey!"

"Miss Gresham!" snapped Ms. Reedy, hurrying over. "What's the problem?"

Rylie spun, baring her teeth. She couldn't even think of what to say. She didn't know how to defend herself. All she could think was *hungry* and—

"She freaked out at me!" complained Kathleen.

Maxine nodded. "It's true. I saw it."

Rylie floundered for human language. "They just—I don't—"

Ms. Reedy pointed at her. "Dean's office. Now."

She didn't wait to be escorted, since she had seen the sign for the dean at the front office that morning. Rylie stormed out of the room as the teacher picked up her phone to alert the office she was on her way.

As soon as she hit the sunshine and fresh air, her head cleared, and she felt a little ridiculous.

What had she been thinking?

The anger vanished before she'd taken three steps away from the building, and she was cold with nerves by the time she reached the dean. The secretary was expecting her. He directed Rylie to a chair in the hallway behind him, and Rylie sat with her face buried in her hands.

"Who are you?"

She took a sniff of the air before checking the source of the drawling voice. She was surprised to pair the sticky-sweet scent of marijuana with the guy sitting on the other end of the hallway. He wore a polo shirt and loafers, and he looked like he fit into the farming community about as well as Rylie did. His hair was even spiked in the front.

"Who are *you*?" Rylie countered.

"I'm Tate. You must have done something good to visit the dean on your first day of school."

"How did you know?"

"I've lived here for longer than a week. I know *everyone*." He kicked his feet up on the opposite chair, cupping his hands behind his head. "So you're Rylie. I saw you on TV."

Of course. Rylie's face had been splashed all over the city back home after she went missing at summer camp. There had been a small media storm when they found her. Just another reason for her to avoid the city.

"I didn't think I made the news this far west," she said.

"You didn't. I spend a lot of time online. So was it really bears?"

"No," she said. On a whim, she added, "It was werewolves."

Tate seemed to find this hilarious. His laugh sounded too feminine coming out of his large frame. "Nice. So, I don't suppose you like four-twenty, do you?"

"What's that?"

"You know. Ganja. Mary Jane."

Rylie snorted. "No. I don't smoke pot."

"Have you tried it? You might have fun, and I'm the only guy in town who sells it," Tate said.

"No thanks. You'll be the first person to hear about it if I change my mind, though." Which Rylie didn't see happening anytime soon. But Tate reminded her a lot of some of her stoner friends back home, so she couldn't help smiling.

He took her rejection with a shrug. "So what did you do to earn a visit to the dean? Piss off Ms. Reedy?"

"Kathleen, actually."

"Nice," he said again. "Nice. I was caught smoking behind the bleachers again. I don't know why it surprises them anymore. What else am I supposed to do in this dump of a town?"

"Vandalism?" she suggested.

Dean Block found them laughing in the hall, and she gave her face a tired rub. "Great," she muttered. "Miss Gresham, please wait in my office. Tate…"

He held up his hands. "I know. Don't do it again."

"Just… wait out here."

Tate gave Rylie a little ironic wave goodbye. She smiled sheepishly.

Everything in the dean's office was brown. The only light came through a tiny window with frosted glass. It was probably supposed to feel warm and cozy, but Rylie felt claustrophobic.

She sat in the chair across from the desk to wait, and the dean came back in after talking to Tate. The circles under her eyes looked even darker after their conversation. "Your aunt is on her way," she said. "She should be here in about a half an hour. Do you want to tell me what happened?"

"No," Rylie said, focusing on the cup of pens on the corner of the desk.

"Ms. Reedy said you picked a fight with Kathleen."

The wolf swelled inside of her, and she clenched her hand into a fist. Her fingernails dug into her palm. "She's the one who started it!"

"I'm sure." Dean Block didn't look impressed. "What happened?"

Rylie opened her mouth to spill—then shut it again. "Nothing."

"If you don't give me your side, then all I can do is take the teacher's story as fact. We may not be some big city school like you're used to, but we do have rules about how we handle this kind of thing, if it's true. You could get a suspension."

"I'm not talking until my aunt gets here."

The dean rubbed her face again. "All right, all right."

Rylie passed the time by stealing a pen out of the cup and doodling curling lines from one corner of a sticky-note to the other. Dean Block worked on the computer, ignoring her completely. She wondered if the silent treatment was supposed to make her nervous. It was working. She had never been in any dean's office before.

A half hour inched past on the clock. Finally, the door opened, and Aunt Gwyn came in. She set her hat on the edge of the desk, then dusted her hands off on her jeans. "Sorry. I've been working all day. I'm a downright mess."

"Thanks for coming. Please take a seat."

Gwyn stayed standing. "Tell me what Rylie did."

"She provoked a fight and threw a book," the dean said. "We understand transitions to new schools are difficult, but—"

Her aunt cut Dean Block off with a hand. "Yeah, I get that. Can we talk in private?"

Uh oh.

"Okay. Miss Gresham, would you wait in the hall?"

Tate was gone, leaving her no distraction from the nerves gnawing in her belly. Rylie bounced her knee as she waited, chewing on her thumbnail until the edge bled. She could imagine the conversation going on inside the office.

You think she's been acting weird? the dean would ask.

Yeah. All the animals are afraid of her. I think something happened at camp. Something really bad, Gwyn would reply.

We're going to expel her.

And Aunt Gwyneth would smile that unsympathetic smile. *Good. I wanted to send her back to her mom anyway.*

The thought of it made her want to scream.

What would happen if someone did realize what happened to Rylie? There was no way anybody would believe it if she told them she was a werewolf, and there was no cure now that she had changed.

No cure... except a silver bullet.

This scene was too familiar to one Rylie had experienced at camp over the summer. She had been caught sneaking over to the boys' camp with a car she stole from the faculty. She only escaped arrest because a counselor stood up for her—and Jericho only did it to keep Rylie under his thumb. He turned out to be a werewolf and hoped she would help him attack the camp.

Gwyn had no ulterior motives. After Rylie's refusal to work that morning, she didn't have much of a reason to keep her niece at all. Even if she didn't get expelled, it seemed like there was a pretty slim chance of getting to stay at the ranch.

She wouldn't live with her mom. She *couldn't*.

When her aunt emerged, Rylie stood up.

"I'm not going back to the city," she said.

Gwyn's expression didn't change. "Of course you're not. Come on, I'm parked out front."

She strode off, leaving Rylie staring after her.

That was it? Wasn't she supposed to get yelled at or something?

Rylie hurried to catch up with her. She got in the passenger's side and buckled her belt silently. Her aunt tuned the radio to a country station and hummed along with it as she drove.

Instead of turning left toward the road that would take them to the ranch, they headed downtown. Rylie couldn't stand the quiet.

"Where are we going?"

"Hardware store," she said. "I told you we would get paint for your room after school, didn't I?"

"You're not going to get rid of me? I thought I was expelled for sure."

"Not this time. The dean's willing to work with your issues." Rylie didn't realize how afraid she'd been until it drained out and left her weak. Gwyn stopped at a traffic light and gave her a hard look. "You're not going to throw anything again. Not books, not temper tantrums. Nothing. You're going to control yourself."

"But—"

"Tomorrow, you're going to wake up and do your chores without complaining. You're going to go to school. You're going to blend in. And you're *not going to get in trouble.*"

"It's just—"

"I'm running a ranch, girl. It's a big job. I can't go running into town every day because you're making trouble. I'll start losing money, which is not an option, so I will send you back to your mother. Understand me?"

Rylie nodded. "I understand."

"Good. Now, what color do you want to paint your room?"

Four

Strangers

By the time Rylie and Gwyn were finished with retail therapy, they had a lot more than paint. A shopping spree in a town with one half-empty strip mall was virtually impossible, but they picked up furniture from an antique store and Rylie scrounged together a few designer outfits from the consignment shop. It wasn't much, but it beat her aunt's hand-me-downs.

They emptied Rylie's bedroom and did the primer coat that night. It was awful to her sensitive nose. She slept on the deck chair with a checkered blanket pulled to her chin, and awoke in the morning damp and chilly.

The days quickly began to take on a strange sort of rhythm: Rylie woke up at four in the morning to eat breakfast (whether she liked it or not), struggled to find chores that kept her away from the animals, and then took the long ride to high school. She didn't dare argue with her aunt anymore. She weeded the garden, repaired fences, and hauled bales of hay. The cows panicked and tried to stampede whenever she passed. Gwyn didn't remark on it, but she never stopped watching.

It got easier after the first day, in the sense that she was no longer a novelty and became part of the scenery. New students weren't interesting gossip for long.

On the other hand, classes with Ms. Reedy didn't get much easier. She hovered over Rylie and watched her every move.

Fortunately, it turned out Tate was supposed to be in Ms. Reedy's class instead of smoking under the bleachers. He strolled in reeking of weed to claim the seat next to Rylie after a few days. He immediately pulled out his phone and started texting.

"Care to share your discussions with the class?" the teacher asked.

"Just planning a drive-by with my gang," he said.

This seemed to be a normal response for him, because Ms. Reedy only looked pained. "Put your phone away, Mr. Peterson."

It was nice having Tate to distract the teacher. She made it through the week without another disruption, and by the second week, Rylie was sitting with Tate and his degenerate friends at lunch. The three of them were repulsive, like every other teenage boy she had ever met, but they were also wonderfully simple creatures. All they cared about were video games and marijuana.

Rylie could almost forget the full moon was coming.

Almost.

"I hear you're hanging out with a bad crowd at school," Gwyn said over a dinner of steaks from her own herd. Considering how much meat her aunt ate, she might as well have been a werewolf too—and she managed to top it off with several steins of beer.

Rylie shrugged. "They're all right."

"Are you doing drugs with them?"

"No."

Her mom would have never accepted that answer without an hour of interrogation, but it was enough for Gwyneth. "Good. You don't work on my ranch if you're not clean."

"Trust me, that's not a problem." Rylie could barely control herself anymore. The idea of throwing substance abuse into the mix was stupid.

The clinking of silverware against plates filled the room for a couple moments. Gwyn set down her fork. The line between her eyebrows said she was thinking hard again.

"I'm going to give it to you straight, babe: You're a great worker. You're almost as strong as both my men combined, so I'm happy to have you. But this refusal to ride my horses is a serious problem. You want to explain it to me?"

"I had a bad experience at camp," she said. "Actually, I had a lot of bad experiences at camp."

Sympathy flashed across Gwyn's hard face. "Yeah. I know."

Rylie ate her last bite of steak and pushed the plate back. She could have probably had two more of them without feeling full. "I'm surprised you haven't tried to play twenty questions about it yet. It was all Jessica wanted to talk about."

"You went missing for two weeks. She was scared for you."

"You weren't?"

"I was, but you're tough. I knew you would be fine. Since you've come back, though, you've been... different. You're darker now. Guess that's no surprise considering what you've been through."

She didn't meet her aunt's eyes. "Yeah."

"If you want to talk about it, I'm here. Until then, there's work to be done." Aunt Gwyn grabbed another beer out of the fridge and sat down, using the side of the table to pop the cap off. She poured it into her glass. "Your sixteenth birthday is coming up soon."

Was it? Rylie had completely forgotten. Time for her was no longer marked by days and weeks and months. It was

All Hallows' Moon

measured out in phases of the moon. "We don't have to do anything."

"Do you want to learn to drive?"

She smiled. "Really?"

"I don't have time to drive an hour into town twice a day. It would be mighty convenient if you could do it yourself. So I'll tell you what, Rylie—if you can get past this summer's bad experience and go for a ride on Butch, I'll teach you to drive. You can even have the old truck."

Her excitement faded. "Oh."

"Just one ride. Saddle him up, take him out with me, and head back. Then you can get your driver's license. How's that sound?"

"I don't think I can do that, Aunt Gwyn," Rylie said.

"Give it some thought." She polished off her beer in one long drink and sighed. "I'm exhausted, babe. Think I'll call it an early night. Why don't you clean up?"

Rylie mulled over her aunt's offer while she washed plates in the sink. If she could ride the horse once, she could drive. None of her friends back in the city could drive. Everyone rode the train. But out in the country, driving meant independence. Adulthood. She could do whatever she wanted, whenever she wanted.

If only she could ride on a horse.

Rylie used to love riding horses. The thought of galloping through the pastures with the breeze in her hair was so tempting that she could almost cry.

But she smelled like a wolf to the animals now. A predator. As soon as they caught a whiff of her, they would panic and bolt.

She couldn't do it.

Rylie put away the dishes and made a halfhearted attempt at homework. It was hard to focus on drawing mitochondria when she kept finding herself doodling moons and paw prints on the margins. Her mind wandered to the horses, and then the transformation coming the next night.

She probably hadn't eaten Phil, the trucker. Rylie would have heard about it if they found his mangled body somewhere. The cows were another story—that one had made it into the newspapers. All the local ranchers were talking about crazy coyotes and mountain lions.

The full moon would be even worse. Rylie would be even hungrier than before.

If she roamed free again, she would probably kill. She couldn't lock herself in the bedroom next to her aunt's. The barn wasn't an option, either, unless she wanted to kill the horses.

Rylie groaned and cradled her head in her palms. She had to do *something*.

If only Seth had been there for her. He'd had all kinds of creative ways to keep her restrained over the summer. Of course, it turned out that was because he was a werewolf hunter, and he killed her kind. But he hadn't wanted to hurt her.

She wondered what he was doing. Was he thinking about the upcoming moon, too?

When night fell, Rylie crept past Aunt Gwyn's room. She had already gone to sleep even though it was only eight o'clock. There was no sound coming from her room. Rylie walked out the front door and kept going.

Her aunt's ranch looked like it had grown out of the long grass in the middle of rolling hills and sweeping plains. Everything was made of round edges: the squash cluttering the unkempt garden, the worn wooden posts forming the fence around the pond, the bodies of the cows milling around the field.

There were no mountains in sight. Not a single jagged edge or towering rock face. That was exactly how Rylie wanted it. She'd had more than her share of mountains over the summer.

Once the house was a black dot on the horizon, Rylie tugged on her skirt's laces and let it puddle on the ground, dropping her camisole on top. Bare to the sky, she shut her eyes and tilted her face back, spreading her arms wide.

The almost-full moon poured silvery rays through her flesh. She felt like it would dissolve into her skin and bones until she was a wraith so she could drift away on the breeze. Rylie wanted to be nothing but a thought lifting amongst the stars, letting her body and the wolf trapped inside of it disappear beneath her.

No more anger. No more violence. No more pain.

But no matter how hard she imagined separating her soul from its vessel, Rylie was anchored to the earth by human feet and human needs and a wolfish impatience that wondered why she was wandering when she should have been resting for the hunt.

Headlights on the road made Rylie cover her body with her arms, even though she didn't think anyone would be able to see her at that distance. Prickles rolled from her hairline down to her spine. Why would someone drive down her desolate stretch of highway at night? Something wasn't right.

The car turned down her aunt's private road… and stopped. The headlights blinked off.

Rylie dropped to a crouch and ran down the hill. She beelined for the car, flashing through the long grass like a pale ghost. It occurred to her that her human skin was whiter than the wolf's fur and that she would be spotted if she didn't move fast. Hanging underneath a shadowy copse of trees to watch the driver, Rylie laid her belly to the ground.

The passenger stepped out of the car. He was tall and smelled horrible. It wasn't like he hadn't showered, because she could also smell his soap and deodorant. There was something else. Something that smelled sour and *wrong*.

Some deep, dark place within her recognized the stench. It made her stomach roil.

The other door opened, and the driver came out onto the side of the road. "Put that away." A woman's voice.

He turned, letting Rylie see that he was holding a rifle. She could make out a sliver of his face. He had a strong jaw and dark eyes. "I thought I heard something."

"You're not shooting anybody tonight. I said, put it away."

A chill rolled through Rylie. She had been hoping these people might be farmers, but something about that tone said they were not. They didn't look like they belonged in her little rural community. Both wore plain clothes in dark colors, and they looked more like soldiers than ranchers.

"We're being watched," the man insisted, and Rylie didn't dare breathe.

"You're imagining things. Get back in the car, Abel. What if the property owner comes out and sees us pointing guns at her cows?"

The rifle lowered. "Do you think the woman who owns the ranch is the one? This Gwyneth Gresham?"

"No. It would have started months ago if she was. Get in the damn car."

The man went to the other side, and Rylie finally saw him. All of him. He might have been attractive once, but a scar bisected his face now, running from one eyebrow to the opposite corner of his mouth. It wasn't as scary as his expression. It was the look of a man who had killed other men and was willing to do it again.

A trickle of fear crept into Rylie's heart. And then, right on cue, her stomach growled. The wolf stirred inside of her at the sight of the scar. It was hungry.

This "Abel" was injured and vulnerable—her favorite thing. She could finish the job. He was probably delicious. Weren't the ones who fought the ones who tasted the best? There was nothing like the chase, and the satisfaction of hunkering down to eat a well-earned meal.

She shuddered and shut her eyes so she wouldn't have to see him anymore. The injury was too exciting. Rylie had never been so fascinated by the thought of someone in pain before, but now it made her heart race.

Rylie slipped back into the shadows as the car returned the main road. Once they were gone, she went home and climbed into bed. Violent thoughts raced through her mind.

She was terrified of what those people might have been looking for, and worse, what she wanted to do to them. She couldn't calm down enough to sleep.

When she finally did, her dreams were filled with blood.

Five

Truancy

Five o'clock in the morning is the worst time possible to chase cattle through knee-high mud, but that was exactly where Rylie found herself on the morning of September eighth.

Rylie had never thought of cows as creatures that could *run*, since they had the dumb expression of black meatballs, but it turned out the proper motivation could get those tubby bodies moving—fast.

"Amazing," laughed Gwyn from her seat on the fence. "You really woke up those cows!"

It seemed like the first logical step to getting on a horse would be to approach other, slower animals, so when her aunt asked if she wanted to milk cows, Rylie agreed. But it was harder than she expected. *Much* harder.

Anger burned in her cheeks. "Are you going to help me or what?"

"Why would I help when I'm having so much fun watching?"

Bitch.

The thought whip-cracked through her mind, and it almost crossed Rylie's lips before she could bite it back. Violent thoughts spilled through her, one after the other: shoving her aunt off the fence, ripping her claws into the cows, tearing out throats, showing her aunt what was *really* fun…

But Rylie couldn't get near the cows as a human, much less maul them. She was too slow. The embarrassment of it didn't calm her fury.

It would be the full moon that night, so Rylie's temper was at its worst, but she didn't dare snap at her aunt again. She would be sent back to the city. She might hurt someone. It was the only thing that kept her from acting on her ugly fantasies.

"I hate this," Rylie said. It was probably the biggest understatement she had ever made.

Gwyn's smile softened. "Yeah, babe. I know." And then she had that impatient look again, and she checked her watch as she hopped off the fence. "Well, that was a good laugh. Let's feed the goats."

"Don't the cows need to be milked?"

Her aunt laughed. "These aren't dairy cows, Rylie! These are *steak* cows! You think people chase cattle to milk them anyway? There are pens and chutes and machines for that."

Rylie went rigid. Her vision blurred. "You mean you were having me chase the cows for *fun?*"

"I enjoyed myself," Gwyn said.

A rumbling growl rose in Rylie's throat, and the remaining cows fled to the other side of the pasture.

Rylie refused to speak to her aunt on the ride into town even though she itched to ask about the people she had seen the night before. She had a feeling they weren't cattle hustlers. "I'm going to get a ride back with one of my friends," she said, hopping out of the truck. "Don't bother getting me."

"All right. Give me a call if you change your mind."

She waited to leave until Gwyn's truck disappeared around the corner.

The school wasn't expecting her that morning. She had already called in sick pretending to be her aunt. It wasn't a complete lie. Rylie never felt good on the day before a moon.

There was no way she would make it through Ms. Reedy's class without eating someone.

But she couldn't hang around town, either. It was too small, and everyone knew each other. Someone would tell her aunt she ditched.

So instead, Rylie ran.

In the days at her mom's condo, Rylie did a lot of research. There wasn't much real information about werewolves online. So she read about normal wolves—the kind that lived in the forest and didn't eat people. She learned that they ran at about five miles per hour and that they could travel fifty miles a day.

Rylie had never pushed herself to see how fast she could go, but she was pretty sure she could beat normal wolves in speed and distance. Even as a human, it felt like she would never get tired.

She wound through the fields toward her aunt's ranch, leaping fences and avoiding the road. It was getting to be harvest time, so there were lots of people working on tractors and other big equipment. A farmer yelled at her, but she was too fast to hear what he said.

It felt good to run. It used up all the high-tension energy of the wolf. She finally passed the last farm and broke into federal park land, where there was nothing but open hills and blue sky.

Rylie was looking for something, but she wasn't sure exactly what. She needed somewhere to hide. Somewhere safe, where nobody would stumble upon her. Where could she hide when the land was so open?

She hoped to find a cave or something, but it quickly became obvious there were no caves in the land of rolling hills even though she searched for hours.

The sun passed its apex and grew hotter. Rylie finally stopped under a tree to drink her water and see what her aunt packed for lunch. Apparently one of the hens had stopped laying eggs, because she had half of a roasted chicken in a

Tupperware container. She tore into it and tried not to dwell much on the fact that it wasn't raw.

Once she was satiated, Rylie lounged under her tree and surveyed the hills around her, picking bits of chicken meat out of her teeth with a rib bone. She had found a few old shacks, but none of them looked like they could hold her.

Rylie pulled out a county map she borrowed from her aunt's house and frowned at it. Normal wolves could travel fifty miles in a day. There were more than fifty miles of emptiness to the north and east of the ranch, but how could she get herself to go that direction once she transformed?

She still had no ideas by the time she packed up her knapsack and went running back for the ranch.

Rylie arrived an hour after school ended. Her aunt and the ranch hands were loading some of the livestock into trailers, so she avoided them to keep the cows from panicking.

Flopping on the floor of her bedroom to wait, Rylie chewed on her bottom lip as she watched the shadows march up her wall. Her skin was dry from the climate. It cracked under her teeth, tasting of salt and iron.

The hours passed and evening settled over the pastures. Rylie sat on the porch after dinner and watched the sun turn to a sliver on the horizon, leaving nothing but a fading orange glow. The animals quieted down. A cloud of mosquitoes swarmed over the rain barrel.

Twilight. She could already feel the moon pulling at her.

Rylie's eyes burned. That tug meant she would change soon. She had come to associate it with the agony of her bones breaking, her skin tearing, and fur swarming over her flesh.

She didn't want to change again. Not tonight, not ever.

Rylie went inside. Her aunt had fallen asleep leaning on the kitchen table with a mug of tea steaming by her hand. Gwyn looked as ragged as Rylie felt. When had her aunt gotten old?

All her anger from that morning was gone. Kneeling by Gwyn's chair, she shook her gently. "Hey. Why don't I help you into bed?"

Her aunt's eyes opened a sliver. She smiled to see Rylie. "I wasn't sleeping."

"Then you fake-snore really good. Come on."

Rylie led her back to her room. Moving slowly across the house felt strange when the wolf part of her was ready to run, but she forced herself to be gentle.

Gwyn wouldn't let her walk her all the way into her room. "I'm fine," she insisted. "Leave me alone." There was no venom in her tone.

"Okay. I'm going to bed too. See you in the morning."

The door shut. Pain rocked through Rylie, and she pressed her forehead to the doorframe.

She had to move fast.

Running was harder with the full moon hanging overhead. Her feet flashed beneath her, but it felt strange to spring on two legs when Rylie wanted to drop to all fours. She stopped once she reached the hill where she had seen the car the night before.

Another swell of power hit her. Rylie's eyes blurred and her ears rang. She stripped her clothes off and stashed them under a bush before continuing. She made it another quarter mile before she lost control.

Her legs gave out. Rylie dropped to her knees and began to transform.

Her vertebrae ground against each other like they were twisting into dust. One popped, and then another. Her tailbone snapped. The skin at the base of her spine stretched and ripped as the tail extended to her knees. Rylie screamed, digging her fingers into the soil.

Make it stop, make it stop—

When she lifted her hands, her fingernails had torn free of her skin and lay on top of the dirt like ten bloody seeds waiting to sprout. Claws emerged. The bones in her wrist rippled and rearranged.

Please just make it stop—

Her kneecaps cracked.

Thick clumps of blond hair puddle beneath her.

Her ribs shifted. Blood sprayed across the ground, splattering in lines on the grass and misting the petals of the flowers.

Rylie sobbed into her fists, but she couldn't make fists anymore, she didn't have fingers—and then she couldn't cry because her lips were gone and her face was *tearing*—

Stop, stop, oh God, just stop…

Fur itched under her skin and erupted from the surface.

And then Rylie was gone.

The wolf felt the completion of the changes, but it was not bothered by the pain. It shook itself, flicking remnants of Rylie's blood across the field. Stretching its paws in front of its body, it extended its body to work out all the kinks.

Rylie had eaten nothing but meat that night, but the moon was full, the wolf was strong, and all it could think about was the gnawing hunger beneath its ribs.

Over its shoulder, the wolf could smell animals. They weren't far away at all.

And it wanted to hunt.

•◐•

Rylie woke up with feathers stuck to her face.

She sat up. Something itched against her gums, and she picked another feather out of the space between her canines and molars. It was big and red. The last time she had seen that feather, it was attached to a rooster.

The chicken pen was completely silent. She crawled to the door of the henhouse and looked inside.

No wonder it was so quiet.

SM Reine

"I'm going to be in so much trouble," Rylie muttered.

She managed to get inside before her aunt woke up and took a long, hot shower. Rylie scrubbed at the chicken blood on her face, chest, and arms with a loofah until her skin turned raw and pink.

All the wolf had left inside the chicken coop were bloody stains. When she tried to remember what she had done with them, she could almost recall the sensation of bones cracking in her jaws, and the feeling of fragments scraping down her throat.

Rylie wanted to feel guilty. Chickens were living creatures deserving of compassion as much as any cow, after all. But when she remembered the rooster's attack on her first morning at the ranch, she felt a little satisfied to have eaten him.

She knew her aunt had woken up when her hot water vanished, and she leaped out of the shower with a yelp. That meant Gwyn was cooking breakfast. Rylie shivered as she toweled off with weak motions. She was drained after the full moon. She couldn't even make herself fake a smile at the breakfast table.

Rylie picked at her bacon while her aunt read the newspaper. She was still full from the night before, so nothing looked edible.

"I've got a lot to do today. I'm going to have to take you into town early," Gwyn said, offering her the section of the newspaper with the comics. She shook her head. "Suit yourself. Is everything ready for school?"

"Yeah."

"All right. Throw your dishes in the sink and we'll go."

Her nerves grew tighter as they walked to Gwyn's truck with her knapsack over her shoulder. They passed the coop. It was too far away to see what Rylie had done, and the henhouse faced in the wrong direction.

All they needed to do was walk five feet to the truck, shut the doors, and drive. Then she would be safe. Gwyn wouldn't find out. She might not notice until…

"Have you heard the rooster this morning?" her aunt asked, stopping at the tailgate of the truck.

Rylie's heart plummeted. "I thought I heard it around sunrise."

Gwyn tilted her head as she listened. Rylie's sensitive ears picked up buzzing flies, but her aunt would hear nothing but silence.

"Hang out here a second," Gwyn said, jogging down the hill. She walked around one side of the coop first, then the other, and then opened the gate to go inside.

Rylie hadn't realized her aunt knew so many swear words. She hurried down to stand on the other side of the chicken wire, hesitating to go inside. She had seen enough dead birds for one day.

"Jesus," Gwyn muttered. "Some coyotes."

She swallowed a burp that tasted like chicken and turned it into an awkward cough. "That's what I told you the other week. Coyotes are really bad around here."

Her aunt gave her a hard stare through the fence. "Do you know anything about this?"

"No."

Even though Rylie didn't sound convincing, it was ridiculously implausible for any human to have caused the carnage in the henhouse, so Gwyn shook her head.

"Let's head to town. Looks like I need to buy some new chicks."

Six

The Newest Student

Rylie didn't notice the passage of time in terms of days or weeks anymore, but the school did. October snuck up on her, and the school was soon draped in orange streamers and grimacing cardboard pumpkins.

She studied the announcements board—which, in a school so small, mostly involved birthdays and straight A report cards—and was surprised to see there would be a party at the end of the month.

For her last Halloween, Rylie had gone to a huge party at Lance Cunningham's house. She dressed up as a sexy nurse and glared at anyone who tried to flirt with her. Tyler had gotten so drunk that he barfed orange Jell-o shots everywhere and had to go to the hospital.

It wasn't her favorite time of year.

This party wouldn't be anything like that, but there would be a costume contest during the lunch period. She rolled her eyes. Rylie hadn't had a costume contest in school since fourth grade.

There were murmurs in the halls when she went to her morning class, but this time, nobody was staring at her. Something—or someone—else had gotten everyone talking.

Rylie didn't care. Grateful for the distraction, she took her usual seat with Tate and tried not to doze off on her text book.

"Did you hear? There's another new student!"

Rylie lifted her head from her paper. She had been doodling a wolf eating a turkey. "Huh?"

"There's another new student," Tate repeated. He didn't bother to whisper even though they were supposed to be taking a quiz. Rylie had gotten three questions done before giving up. "That means two of you in one year. It's too exciting for the small-minded rabble in this urinal of a school."

"Is he our age?"

"Naw. He's a senior." Tate's expression went dreamy. "I wonder if he likes to smoke."

Rylie snorted.

She barely got through the quiz by the time the bell rang. She dropped her packet on the teacher's desk, and Tate did the same, although his was completely blank other than a drawing of a pot leaf on the first page.

There were clouds on the horizon when they went to eat lunch on the quad. Tate's friends were already at their usual bench, and Rylie got the impression they had never gone to class. One of them was too busy with his laptop to look up, but the other gave her a nervous smile before going back to his video game magazine.

She half-listened to her idiot friends talking about games while eating lunch. Two new students in a year. That would have been unremarkable back home, but it seemed unlikely in such a small town. Rylie had a bad feeling about it, but she wasn't sure why.

Someone walking across the quad caught the wolf's attention. His gait was strange. He was swinging on crutches with one leg in a brace below the knee.

"Who's that?" she asked, interrupting Tate in the middle of a tirade about evil corporations assimilating small video game developers.

He glanced over. "Oh, him? That's the new guy. Picked a good time to break his leg, huh?"

She glanced around to make sure nobody was watching before shutting her eyes and taking a deep sniff. Even without her eyesight, she could vividly envision the quad. The two kids leaning against the tree had sex that morning in the locker room. The girl over there was on her period. Half of the people had been eating cafeteria pizza, and the other half were eating leftovers, nachos, Funyuns, cookies, or a dozen other types of junk food. A slight breeze from a passing group tickled the hairs on her arms. She could tell it was the football team by their sweat.

Picking out the smell of the injured boy wasn't hard. "I'll see you guys in English," Rylie said, picking up her knapsack and following the scent trail.

The boy moved fast considering his handicap, but she was faster. He went into the cafeteria, where all the food smells would making tracking harder, so Rylie closed the gap between them.

When he opened the door to the multipurpose room, the blowing air wafted his smell in her direction. Her nose twitched. Rylie smelled something familiar—something she hadn't expected to ever encounter again.

The boy with the cast kept moving toward the doors on the opposite end of the building. He slowed down as he struggled with his crutches. The sight of such easy prey made the wolf stir, but Rylie suppressed her violent thoughts.

She took another sniff of his trail.

No way.

She recognized those broad shoulders and that dark hair. Even better, she recognize the smell of gunpowder and leather that always hung around him, even though he wasn't carrying a gun or wearing his leather jacket.

He stopped at the door and took an arm off one of the crutches to push it open. She stopped behind him and found the strength to speak.

"Seth?"

He turned, and Rylie couldn't breathe.

It was Seth, just as she remembered him. His hair was shorter now, but nothing else had changed. He wore his usual uniform of a black t-shirt and jeans. She had only seen him wearing something else once or twice.

They looked at each other. A moment of blank confusion flashed across his face, and then he dropped his crutches.

"*Rylie?*"

She didn't remember crossing the space between them. All of a sudden she found herself wrapping her arms around him, and he was holding her, and for the first time in months Rylie felt right.

Burying her face in his neck, she took deep breaths of his skin without caring how weird it must look to the other students. The smell behind his ear was rich and earthy with the tang of steel around the edges. Rylie wanted to melt into him.

"You're *alive*," Seth said, leaning back to search her face.

"Are you hurt? Your leg wasn't... I mean... I didn't do anything to you, did I?"

His smile faltered. "You don't remember?"

"Everything that happens when I change is still kind of hazy. I had no idea what happened to you. I thought you were..." Rylie trailed off, unwilling to finish the sentence.

"It was Jericho," he said in a voice barely above a whisper. "You stopped him before he could kill me. I got lucky."

"Did he bite you?"

"No. He didn't even break my leg, actually, and I had almost completely healed, but then I was practicing some moves with my brother and... What am I saying? Rylie, what are you doing here?"

"I'm going to school," she said. "I've moved in with my aunt, who has a ranch about fifteen miles out of town. I didn't think the city would be safe for someone like me. There's a lot more room in the country. What are *you* doing here?"

Realization dawned in his eyes, and his hands dropped from her shoulders, leaving her cold.

"Oh no. This is bad. This is *really* bad."

"What?"

Even though it didn't look like anyone was watching, Seth put a finger to his lips to silence her. "Not here. Follow me."

Seth picked up his crutches and limped outside to the tree. Its roots sprawled across the ground in thick knots, and leaves showered around them with every gust of wind.

"We came to hunt," he said in a low voice. His dark eyes glimmered like coals. "Me and my brother and my mom. We keep an eye on the news for signs of werewolves, like weird attacks on livestock. When we saw what happened to the herd here, we jumped on it."

"You're here to... oh." Hunt werewolves.

Hunt *Rylie*.

She remembered Seth telling her about his family, but she had never met them. It made too much sense now. His brother had been attacked by a werewolf and almost transformed. That trespasser with a mangled face was Seth's brother, that woman was his mom, and they were here to hunt.

Seth's family wanted to kill her.

He looked grim. "I said it was bad."

"I've only been here for a couple of weeks," Rylie said.

"But you killed those cows, didn't you?"

Rylie focused on a line of ants marching across the roots of the tree. She shouldn't have been so embarrassed. Seth had already seen her at her worst when she slaughtered a deer, but she hated having him know she wasn't controlled.

"They belonged to my aunt," she said.

He didn't reply for so long that she finally met his solemn gaze. She couldn't read his expression. "You have to leave."

"No. Your family needs to leave, Seth."

"This isn't the right place to have this talk. Why don't I come see you after school? We'll talk about it at your aunt's house."

"Sure. Her address is—"

"I know where you live, Rylie," he said. He looked uncomfortable. "My brother was scoping it out." Seth's hand traced a line down her cheek, and she closed her eyes to savor his touch. "What happened to you after that night at camp?"

"I'm not sure," she said. "I woke up alone. Where were you?"

Seth's fingers dropped to her hand. "I looked for you, but I thought you didn't make it." A hint of that easy smile curved his lips. "I've thought about you every day."

Footsteps approached, and a man spoke. "Are you going to introduce me, Seth?"

He pulled his hand back quickly, and ice shot through Rylie's veins. The newcomer looked like Seth, but taller and older, like he might have been in college. His facial scarring wasn't as scary in the daylight. The shadows of night had twisted his face into something more monstrous.

But even with a smile just like Seth's, Rylie could remember seeing Abel on the road in the dark, holding a rifle loaded with silver bullets.

"Oh yeah," Seth said. He sounded totally normal. How could he be so casual standing between a werewolf and a hunter? She felt like she was going crazy. "Rylie, this is my brother, Abel. Abel, this is Rylie. She's a friend of mine."

"You make friends fast, little man," Abel said. It stretched his scar when he smiled.

She could imagine raking her claws down his flesh, leaving him ragged and screaming. That was how he had gotten the scar in the first place, wasn't it?

Rylie gazed at him mutely, unsure of what to say.

"She's helping me get around school," Seth said.

Abel held her gaze, challenging her to keep staring at his scar. "That's awfully nice of you, Rylie, but I don't think Seth will need help much longer. We're going to the doctor to get his cast removed right now."

She finally dropped her eyes.

"That's great," she mumbled.

"Come on, bro," Abel said, taking Seth's backpack. "Let's get going."

Seth flashed a smile. "See you later, Rylie."

I know where you live.

The more she thought about it, the more menacing that sounded.

Rylie's concentration was wasted for the rest of the day. She could only stare out the windows at the sweeping landscape and think of Seth. What were the odds that a guy she met at summer camp would come to her new school in the same year?

She supposed he odds were actually pretty good, if that guy happened to be a werewolf hunter, and she was a werewolf. It hadn't occurred to Rylie that people might see the news about the cows and connect the attacks to her.

Rylie had to excuse herself from chemistry. She knelt in the handicapped stall of the girl's bathroom and pressed her hands to her forehead to hold in the throbbing ache that settled behind her eyes.

The same sentence kept running through her mind over and over again: *They came to kill me. They came to kill me.*

She was lucky it was the day after her transformation, because the werewolf was exhausted and silent. Her adrenaline ran high. On any other day, Rylie was sure it would have come raging out to do damage.

Her eyes burned and hot tears rolled down her cheeks.

They came to kill me.

It was one thing for him to *tell* her that he hunted werewolves, and another to have him come after her.

Had he been out there last night with Abel? Had they been looking for signs of another attack as they tracked her across the farmlands? If she had gone the wrong way and stumbled across them, would they have shot and skinned her and mounted her head on their wall?

Hysterics rolled through her, and now that she had started crying, she couldn't stop. Her whole body shook. Rylie smothered her sobs against her arms.

She wanted to be happy to see Seth, but instead, she felt betrayed.

Seven

Family

Rylie didn't make it back to chemistry. She sat in the bathroom soaking paper towels in water, rolling them into balls, and flinging them at the ceiling hard enough to stick. When a girl came in to use the toilets, Rylie glared at her with fierce golden eyes until she left again.

She managed to compose herself enough to attend her last class, but she still couldn't focus. The teacher noticed. Rylie saw him whispering with Dean Block at the end of the day.

When she and her aunt got home, there was a message blinking on their answering machine. Rylie knew it had to be about her, but she left the room so she wouldn't have to listen to it with Gwyn.

"Are you having a hard time adjusting?" her aunt asked later.

Rylie made herself smile. "No. I'm happy. I love it here." She couldn't have sounded less enthusiastic if she tried.

"All right. Do you have much homework tonight?" she asked, letting her niece's obvious lie slide past without remark. Rylie shook her head. "Then I need you to work in the garden. The boys and I are taking some cattle to auction, and the squash are ready. Get the weeds while you're at it."

She nodded, happy to have a distraction, and took a trash bag out to the garden.

Rylie put on gloves and tugged at the weeds halfheartedly. It was a beautiful day to work outside, but she couldn't make herself focus on anything but the memory of Abel's scarred face stretching into a smile.

A cloud of dust rose on the road. Rylie shielded her eyes against the dropping sun to see who approached. She was just wondering why someone with a motorcycle would visit her aunt when Seth came up the hill and stopped on the other side of the garden.

He took off his helmet as he dismounted. His hair stuck up in the back. "Hey," Seth said.

Rylie felt a smile growing, and she ducked her head to hide it. How could she be so excited and so scared to see him all at once? "How's your leg?" she asked.

"Perfect. I'm a fast healer."

"I didn't know you can ride motorcycles." Was that a holster for a shotgun on the back? Rylie wasn't sure if that was awesome or terrifying.

Seth looked embarrassed. "I don't have a license. It belongs to my brother. He lets me borrow it sometimes."

He ran a hand through his rumpled hair as he floundered for words.

They spoke at the same time.

"What are you going to do?" she asked, just as he said, "You have to leave."

She bit her lip. "I don't have anywhere else to go. You know why I can't go back to my mom. This is pretty much all I have left."

"Then go somewhere else. Somewhere far away. I have a little money, so I can buy you a bus ticket."

"It's not a money thing. My dad left plenty of money for me when he died. But I'm only fifteen! I can't live alone. I can't even drive a car yet."

Seth looked serious. Very serious. "You'll die if you don't."

A chill settled over her, and it wasn't the breeze. Rylie buried her spade in the ground. "Tell them to call off the hunt."

"Call it off?"

"Yeah. Tell them I'm different and harmless and that you guys can't hunt me."

He laughed humorlessly. "Harmless? You killed those cows."

"So do you think that means I should die?"

"No! Jesus, Rylie." Seth all but collapsed beside her, pain twisting his face. "I know you're different. You had the chance to kill me when you first changed, and you didn't. I've never seen a werewolf show mercy. They *can't* do it. You're... special..."

Her face felt hot. "Tell them that."

"They won't listen to me." He rubbed the leg that had been in a cast earlier. She wondered if it still hurt. "My mom's... intense."

"But you're going to tell them about me, right?" she pressed.

"If I say you're a werewolf, they'll kill you on the next moon. No. I'm not going to tell them. They can't find out."

Rylie flung her spade to the ground and walked away from him. "I already hate your stupid family."

He followed her and grabbed her arm. "Don't do that." She didn't turn around. She was angry, and she could feel the sleepy wolf starting to react to it.

"Why are you here, Seth?" she asked.

"You know why. Look at me, Rylie." When she didn't face him, he tugged on her elbow. "Come on."

It was hard being so close to him. He was even cuter than she remembered. "What?"

"My brother never graduated high school. When he does odd jobs, he has to be a janitor or a road worker or something.

My mom didn't finish third grade. I don't want to be like them—I want to go to college."

"Then do it," she said.

"They're fighting me about it. They want me to hunt, so they think school is a waste of time. English or computer science or whatever isn't going to kill werewolves."

"So what? You're almost eighteen. You can do whatever you want to do."

"It's not that easy. My whole family hunts from the day we can walk. Look at this." He lifted his shirt to show her his back. Scars striped across his spine. "This one nearly paralyzed me. I was thirteen."

Rylie flinched. "Seth..."

He rolled up his pant leg. His right calf below the knee was a mess of white tissue, like thick worms frozen in the middle of burrowing through his skin. She realized he had never worn shorts at summer camp, and now she saw why. "This was a year ago."

"I would never do that to you," she said.

"I know. But this is what it means to be in my family. So you have to get out of here."

"There's got to be an alternative," Rylie said. "What could I do to make them give up?"

"You have to be dead," he said flatly.

"Okay, *besides* that. Would they stop looking for me if it seemed like I disappeared? Like, if they couldn't find me for a few months, would they move away to hunt a different werewolf?"

"They'll never give up." But Seth was obviously thinking about it. His eyes went distant. "Unless... maybe... if they thought you left the area. They would look for you somewhere else. But in order to do that, you'd need to stay quiet for months."

She lifted her chin stubbornly. "I can do that."

But she wasn't really so sure. She was as disconnected from the behavior of the wolf as she was from Abel. She couldn't control herself. She barely even felt human in between moons.

"It might work," Seth said. "But it's dangerous. You know what I think you should do."

A noise in the fields drew Rylie's attention to the pastures. Her aunt and the workers were moving the truck toward the road. "You should go," Rylie said.

He reached out like he was going to take her hand again, but then he thought better of it. "Yeah."

"I guess I'll see you at school."

"Okay. Be careful." Seth got on the motorcycle again, pulling the helmet over his head, and she let herself appreciate the view as he turned it the other way. His arms were really strong, and his back was broad and muscular.

Memories of seeing him swimming shirtless at the lake flitted through her mind. It had been too dark to see his scars. Would she have been as attracted to him if she'd known how damaged he was from the beginning?

The wolf stirred at the thought of his injuries, and Rylie felt ashamed. The truth was that she found him *more* attractive with those scars. But she wasn't sure if it was love, lust, or a very different kind of craving for flesh.

Life was so much simpler over the summer, before she knew the truth about Seth. All she had to worry about was staying human.

Now she had to worry about getting killed.

He gave a wave as he rode off. Rylie gnawed on her lip. She could tell by the way he turned at the end of the road that he must have been staying in town somewhere, since there was nothing else in that direction but farms.

She knew so little about Seth that she couldn't resist. Getting to see his family, and where he lived, would be like getting to peek at her presents on Christmas.

Although she didn't have a car, the road meandered through the hills toward civilization. Rylie could cut straight across the hills and reach town before he did. Gwyn was too busy to pay her any attention, so she shucked her gloves and broke into a run.

Wolves were built for stamina rather than speed, so Rylie had to pace herself. She kept an eye on the road as she ran and spotted him when he took the first exit before town.

Rylie stopped at the turnoff, panting hard and dripping sweat. Her lungs wheezed with the dry air.

His motorcycle had vanished into a gated area marked by a sign: Shady Glen Park. Seth's family was living in a trailer park. Well, that wasn't a big deal... was it? They moved around a lot to hunt werewolves, so what did Rylie expect? A mansion in the suburbs?

She had never been in a trailer park before. The worst neighborhood she visited in the city was the art district, where people lived off royalty checks and gallery sales and struggled to make ends meet. It was hardly the ghetto.

Sneaking in behind the next car, she followed it along the street in search of Seth.

A lot of the trailers were falling apart. Weeds grew through the walls in a few places. One person had a bunch of tires stacked in their front yard. Another person had an upside-down couch in their driveway. The sun reflected off roofs made of tin and made the entire place glow like it was smoldering.

A dog on a short chain growled at her until she turned her gaze on it. Its ears flattened to its skull and it crept backward, hiding behind the half dead tree to which it was tethered.

Rylie hurried to find Seth's motorcycle and spotted it in the back. His mobile home was in better condition than the others, but that might have been because it had been unoccupied for awhile. The FOR SALE sign had "Sold!" stamped across it.

The door stood open, so Rylie hung back on the other side of the street to listen. The home across from theirs was still vacant. She crouched in the shadow of a bush.

It was easy to pick their voices out from amongst the barking dogs and blaring music elsewhere in the community. Seth's family was the only one talking about death.

"...murders going years back, but it's the same thing you always see in a tiny town. I don't think it's her." A woman's voice. She sounded old and tough, like Rylie thought a war veteran might sound. "This wolf's a new transplant."

"Are you sure?" It was Seth talking this time. His voice made her stomach feel funny.

"No, I'm not sure, or else we'd be tracking down this thing right now. What are you doing? Where have you been?"

"I was at school, Mom. And then the doctor."

Rylie didn't get a chance to hear her response. A car passed, and she shrunk back to avoid being noticed.

When the sound of its engine faded, Seth was talking again.

"I told the doctor that the injury was two months old. The fracture didn't show up on the x-rays, so he believed me."

Her chuckle made it sound like she didn't really care. There was motion beyond the slats of the mini-blinds, and Rylie glimpsed a dark-skinned woman walk past. "Get over here and help me scrap together some silver. I'm going to cast bullets tonight."

Silver bullets. A rush of panic swept over Rylie.

Before she could decide how to react, another car approached—and this one was driven by Abel.

Rylie recognized it as a Chevy Chevelle. Jake, one of her friends back home, had been nuts about muscle cars. He would have died for this one. It was a beautiful shade of dark blue with chrome trim, and she could smell the clean leather interiors when he opened the door.

Abel came out with a bag of fast food clutched in his fist. He had peeled the buns off one burger and was eating the three cheese-smothered patties bare. She was embarrassed to have her stomach growl.

He had almost been turned into a werewolf too. There was always a chance that someone bitten wouldn't change if they had enough willpower. Rylie chose to transform so she could save Seth, but Abel fought it back and saved himself. Even so, it looked like he hadn't shaken some of the werewolf's habits, and that included compulsive carnivorism.

When he went inside, the woman's voice grew more affectionate. "Abel. News?"

All three of them moved to a different part of the mobile home so that Rylie couldn't hear what they were saying. She crossed the street, trying to look casual even though she felt out of place in her designer clothes.

She waited by an open window, straining to pick out more than the occasional word. It sounded like they were whispering.

Rylie heard their back door open and swing shut again. Someone had left. She couldn't see who it was from that side of the trailer. Easing around the end, she peeked into the deepening darkness with her ears perked.

And then someone spoke behind her.

"What are you doing?"

She whirled to find Seth at her back. He smelled more strongly of gunpowder than usual. She could tell by a bulge that there was a gun under his shirt—a loaded gun.

"Seth," she said. Guilt formed a lump in her throat.

"Did you follow me here?"

She opened her mouth to lie, but she couldn't think of a convincing way to deny it. She turned her gaze to her feet and nodded. "I was curious."

Grabbing her arm, Seth dragged her behind a tree and pressed her back against the trunk. He peered around her shoulder at his trailer as if to make sure nobody could see them. "Are you suicidal?" he whispered.

She lifted her chin stubbornly. "It's not like they would shoot me on sight."

"They're not dumb. If Abel starts asking questions and finds out you were at Camp Silver Brook this summer, he'll know you're the werewolf." Seth's fingers tightened on her arms. "And you don't want my mom to know you exist."

"Maybe it wouldn't be like that," she said softly.

He didn't try to argue with her. "Look, Rylie... we probably shouldn't be talking to each other."

"Why?"

"I just think it's better if I don't see you for awhile."

"How long?" Rylie asked. There was a rushing sound in her ears that turned his voice distant and foggy, like they were talking from opposite sides of a wall.

"Maybe forever."

Her knees weakened, and she caught herself on the tree. "But this summer..." They had kissed once. She tried not to think about it after that, since she thought she wouldn't see him again, but she thought it might be different since they were back in the same place.

"It was different then." Seth lowered his voice. "You're a werewolf now. I hunt werewolves."

She felt numb. Even the wolf was dumbstruck. "But I changed into a werewolf to save you. It's not my fault."

"I should go back inside, and you should go home, Rylie. Your aunt will miss you."

Seth hung nearby, like he wanted to say something else, but then he went back into the mobile home. The door creaked as it shut behind him.

She made out his mom's voice from inside. "Was someone out there?"

His response was perfectly clear. "No. There's nobody."

Rylie didn't realize she had wandered out of the trailer park until she found herself halfway home. She didn't remember running, and she didn't feel winded. But she did feel like she had been squeezed by a juicer, leaving nothing but a beaten pulp.

The anger struck a moment later.

I changed for him.

Rylie stood in a copse of trees, and she glared at them as though they all had Seth's face with her fists clenched.

I became a monster for him!

With a roar, Rylie tore a sapling from the earth and threw it as hard as she could. Dirt showered from its roots. It crashed into another tree, which cracked at the impact.

Balling her fists into her hair, she dropped to her knees and screamed at the sky.

The wolf was awake now.

And it was furious.

Eight

The Watcher

Gwyn didn't let Rylie rest that weekend. They had to get the ranch ready for winter, which meant (amongst many other chores) digging a ditch along the west side of the barn.

"The runoff last year caused flooding," her aunt explained over a breakfast of chicken-fried steak. "We need to make sure it diverts down to the creek this year. Cows hate swimming. You'll work with Raymond to get that done today."

"Fine," she snapped. "Whatever. Does that mean I get to drive heavy equipment?"

She understood Gwyn's laugh to mean "no," which was how Rylie found herself in the fields with one of the ranch hands and a shovel.

She held it away from her body like it was a giant snake. "You have got to be kidding me," she said.

Raymond was too busy digging to respond. A thick pair of leather gloves protected his hands and a hat shaded his lined face from the sun.

The other ranch hand and Gwyneth were stocking the sheds in anticipation of a long, harsh winter. It had been a drought year, and much of their hay was yellow and dry, but it was better than running out in the middle of a blizzard. Since her aunt wasn't watching, she couldn't force Rylie to work.

She dropped her shovel and sat down on the fence, folding her arms.

Rylie caught a flash of disapproval on Raymond's face. It was enough to set the wolf within her growling, and she didn't have the patience to calm the beast that day. School had been hard after her confrontation with Seth. She kept running across him in the halls, and he would barely look at her, much less stop to talk.

She didn't want to talk to him anyway. She didn't need him in her life. He wanted to hang out with his family? Fine. That was just fine. And the fact that they all wanted to kill her was fine, too. She didn't like them anyway. If Seth wasn't going to help her avoid them, she would take care of them herself.

Sniffling hard, she wiped her nose on the back of her hand.

But why didn't Seth want to be with her?

Raymond grunted as he worked, getting sweaty even though the air was cool enough for them to wear sweaters. There were clouds creeping over the distant hills. It looked like it might snow soon.

"You know your aunt wanted you to help," he said.

"Don't talk to me."

He didn't push, and Rylie tried to ignore his annoyed glances. He was just some guy working for her aunt. He didn't matter.

Raymond was good at what he did, though. He had soon dug a deep hole in the soft earth, piling the castoff earth along the sides. The ranch hands had already started digging a ditch earlier in the week, so he was halfway across the barn in an hour or two. Rylie picked at her fingernails.

He was angry. She could smell it on the air. Why wouldn't he mind his own business?

She could imagine what he was thinking. He probably thought she was an entitled little princess who hadn't done a day of hard work in her life. Rylie bristled. What did he know about her anyway? Nothing!

If he didn't stop looking at her like that, she would claw the eyeballs out of his skull.

His back faced her, but she could feel his disapproval. Gwyn was nowhere to be seen. Nobody would know if she took care of him.

Entitled little princess.

As if she hadn't fought for her life all summer. As if she hadn't been fighting for sanity every day ever since. As if she hadn't been the one to beat the werewolf at camp when nobody else could do it.

She glared holes in the back of his head. "What do you know?" she hissed.

"What?" Raymond asked, straightening.

"Nothing."

He leaned on the handle of his shovel. "You know, I'm not going to get this done today without help."

Help? He wanted *help*?

"Fine," she bit out. "I'll help you."

The shovel was satisfyingly heavy in her hands. She positioned herself behind Raymond and stuck it in the earth, hauling out a clump of dirt. It was easy. She was so strong that she thought she could have dug a ditch around the entire ranch.

She dug for a few minutes without speaking, but Raymond was still looking at her. He was trying to hide it. He was still *thinking* about her, and it made her feel angry and hot and itchy all over, like something was boiling under her skin.

Rylie would *help* him all right.

She swung her shovel deliberately wide as she lifted it, and it smacked into the back of Raymond's shoulders.

He pitched forward with a shout.

Something *crunched* when he landed in the ditch.

Rylie slid down to stand beside him. He was panting, covered in sweat, and grabbing his leg. She thought his ankle might be broken.

"Get—get help—" Raymond groaned, face screwed up with pain. His shovel was a few feet away. He was defenseless.

Her head tilted to the side as she studied him, and Rylie licked her lips.

Delicious.

Someone came running across the field. "Hey! What happened?" It was the other ranch hand, Jorge. He shoved the hat off his head and jumped into the ditch.

Rylie's reverie shattered, and she realized she had been standing over him for at least a full minute while he writhed in pain. She took several steps back to give Jorge space. "It was an accident," she said, hoping her quavering voice made it sound like she was upset. "I accidentally hit him with my shovel, and he fell in."

"Hold still," Jorge said when Raymond tried to stand. "Hey! Gwyneth! Over here!"

Gwyn came down to examine the ranch hand. "We better not move you," she decided. "We'll get an ambulance. Rylie, go to the house and call the hospital."

"It was an accident," she whispered.

"That's not the issue right now, babe. Go call the hospital. The number is on the wall by the phone."

Rylie nodded, clambering out to make the call. Her hands shook when she dialed. It turned out that the hospital was in another town, and they only had one ambulance. It took a long time for them to arrive.

Gwyn and Rylie stood back as Raymond was loaded onto a stretcher. He didn't look good. All the blood had drained from his face, leaving him a ghostly shade of white.

That night, Raymond called them from the hospital. Gwyn set down the phone with a sigh after they spoke and cracked open another beer. That was never a good sign. "Is he going to be okay?" Rylie asked.

"Eventually. He broke a couple of bones and his head almost got knocked off his shoulders, but he's strong. He'll recover." She shook her head. "This is a really bad time of year to lose a man. I'm going to have to hire someone new as soon as possible."

Maybe the next one won't be such a jerk.

Rylie quashed the thought.

"I'm sorry," she said, trying to make it sound like she meant it. "I don't know what happened."

"You need to be more careful, babe. This is a working environment. It's a dangerous place. You need to pay close attention to what you're doing, all right?"

"I just don't think I'm cut out for physical labor," Rylie said.

"You need more discipline. That's all." Gwyn pressed the glass bottle to her forehead and shut her eyes. "I'm too tired for this conversation. I've got a lot to think about. Money is too tight for another employee if we help pay Raymond's bills, but... well, we'll figure something out."

The guilt Rylie hadn't felt earlier crept up on her now. "I'm sorry." She meant it this time.

She worked hard for the next few days without complaining. Gwyn pulled out the heavy machinery (and admitted that she had only made Rylie dig with a shovel as an exercise in patience), and they finished digging the trenches.

Soon, all that remained was moving the animals to different pastures. "But that's going to have to wait until I get a new man," Gwyn said, taking the keys back from Rylie.

"Any responses to your ad yet?"

"A few. There's always someone looking for a job in this economy. I'll be interviewing guys tomorrow."

They didn't get up early Monday morning to work like they usually did. When Rylie got out of bed, she found her aunt asleep on her desk with a checkbook and receipts scattered around her. There was a lot of red ink.

Rylie wasn't helping. Not at all.

She cooked breakfast for herself, waiting to wake Gwyn up until she needed to get to school. The driver's license came creeping up in the back of her mind again. If she could drive, her aunt would have more time. Rylie wouldn't be bothering her as much.

But she couldn't do it. How was she supposed to control herself enough to ride a horse if she couldn't even keep herself from hitting someone with a shovel?

There was a motorcycle Rylie recognized outside the house when they got home from school in the afternoon.

"He's here!" Gwyn said, looking pleased.

"Who?"

"The new guy I hired. I picked him out this morning. You want to meet him?"

Rylie's heart skipped a beat. Was the new hire Seth? "Sure."

A tall figure faced the fields with his back toward them. His hands were stuffed into his pockets. A breeze wafted his scent in her direction, and the hair on the back of her neck lifted.

"This is our replacement ranch hand. His name is—"

"Abel," Rylie said.

His smile might have been charming if it didn't split his mouth in half. "Afternoon, ladies. So nice to see you again." His breath smelled like blood, and he stank of rival wolves. She felt a jolt deep within herself. Did he feel the same thing? Did he realize what it meant?

The werewolf who had bitten Rylie had done it because he wanted a family. Wolves weren't meant to live alone. The werewolf inside of her saw what he was and longed for it. But Abel wasn't really a werewolf—and they could never be pack.

"How do you know each other?" Gwyn asked.

Rylie didn't respond. She was ready for a fight. He was, too—he had his feet spread apart with his arms loose at his sides, and she could see tension coiled in his muscles. Abel was just on edge as she was, even though he smiled with those dark, gleaming eyes.

How much did he know?

"Rylie is friends with my brother. In fact, you could say I only knew about this ranch—and this job—because of her."

He knew.

She tried to keep the shock off her face.

"Well, good." Gwyn gave a sharp nod. "Then we don't need to waste time with introductions." She addressed Rylie. "I'm drawing up a contract for six weeks. He'll help us get everything ready for winter."

"Six weeks?" Rylie asked.

"I'll probably be done in town by then anyway." His smile was frigid.

"Come inside, Abel. We'll go over paperwork and get right to work."

They went into the house. Rylie wanted to shout and stop them. He killed people—even if they were monsters two nights a month. She couldn't leave her aunt with him.

Rylie watched through the kitchen window as they signed papers. They were talking like everything was normal. Like this wasn't the worst idea ever.

Abel must have suspected that she was the werewolf, or he wouldn't be there. Seth once told her that they never killed werewolves while they were in human form. They waited until the transformation. It wasn't much of a comfort now that he was going to be working for her aunt.

She went into her room and shut the door. After a moment of thought, she leaned her dresser against the door.

Rylie hid for the rest of the day, but she couldn't stay in her room forever. Even though Abel left that afternoon, he came back the next day, and the next, and Gwyn would only put up with Rylie's avoidance for so long. There was work to be done.

Which meant that she saw Abel first thing in the morning and after school.

Every single day.

She had to admit that Abel was good to have around. He was at least as strong as Rylie, but the animals weren't afraid of him, so he could get a lot more done. He seemed like he really knew what he was doing, too. But he didn't let his work around the ranch distract him from what seemed to be his true purpose: watching Rylie.

Abel wasn't obvious about it. He was too good for that. He would be standing by the barn when she went to check on the new chicks under the incubator, or he'd be waiting by the compost pile when she took the scraps from dinner out.

If she opened her mouth to ask what he was doing, he walked away as casually as if he hadn't been watching at all. It was too frustrating.

She even caught him watching her at school a few times when she crossed the buildings between classes. His car, with its darkened windows, would idle in the parking lot for hours. Even though she couldn't see him inside of it, she could smell him.

It got to the point where Rylie was constantly looking over her shoulder for him. She couldn't relax. She kept expecting to hear a gunshot and feel a bullet plant itself between her shoulder blades.

"Hey Rylie, are you—"

She jumped and almost fell out of her chair at the library. Kathleen took a quick step back to avoid getting hit.

"What do *you* want?" she snarled.

Kathleen's eyes went wide. "We're supposed to be working on a project together."

Was she spying for Abel? Was she following Rylie the places he couldn't go? Was she a hunter, too? The thoughts raced wildly through Rylie's mind, and she had to struggle to calm down.

"The project, huh?" Rylie asked. "What kind of excuse is that?"

"You could just say you don't want to work on it!" Kathleen hugged her books to her chest and ran away. Rylie let her forehead thud onto the table.

What was wrong with her? The other students weren't spying for Abel. Rylie was sure of that... probably. But she watched the people watching her, and she wondered.

Seth was quiet at school, so she never heard rumors about him. The gossip mill soon got bored of him and started focusing on Rylie again, whose erratic behavior was a popular subject. The only thing that came up about Seth was that the track team was trying to enlist him.

The kind of rumors circulating around Rylie, on the other hand, were much juicier. Popular theory was that she was a drug addict. Her association with Tate wasn't doing anything to discourage it.

"Who cares if you are into drugs anyway? Screw 'em," he said, lighting a joint beneath the bleachers during PE. Rylie hid in the shadows next to him with her knees hugged to her chest. She was wondering if she could see Abel's headlights lurking at the back of the parking lot.

"I don't want those rumors getting back to my aunt," Rylie said. "She'll send me away if she thinks I'm taking something."

"You're worrying too much. Sounds like you need a little help relaxing." He offered the joint to her, but she pushed his hand away.

"No thanks."

Someone walked past the bleachers, and she almost leaped out of her skin.

But it wasn't Abel—it was Seth.

He was wearing his gym uniform, which should have looked stupid on his thick muscles, but he managed to make the sweat pants and t-shirt look like armor. He paused to look at Rylie and Tate sitting shoulder to shoulder under the bleachers.

Unhappy pheromones radiated off of him and his dark eyes glowed. Rylie sat up, bumping her head on a metal bar. "Ouch! Seth, what are you—"

He strode away before she could reach him.

"What's his problem?" Tate asked a moment too late, trying to focus his blurry eyes on Seth's retreating figure.

Her stomach plummeted. *Great.* Now Seth was going to think she was a stoner, too. She shouldn't have cared about his opinion anymore, since he had been the one to say they shouldn't talk, but she did care. A lot. And she was humiliated.

On their drive home that day, Gwyn spoke animatedly about improvements around the ranch and how helpful Abel was to have around. "He's like having four ranch hands! I can't believe how hard this guy works. I might extend his contract after the six weeks have finished."

Her aunt might as well have announced she was going to sign Rylie up for daily root canals.

"Great," she muttered. "Fantastic."

Rylie was writing an essay on the porch when Abel came by for the evening. They were working constantly during daylight now that the nights were getting longer, and he took on the extra hours with enthusiasm.

She tried to ignore him and focus on her paper, which was one of many required for her project with Kathleen, but all of her senses jangled at his presence. He watched her from the bottom of the hill, and the wolf hated it. For once, Rylie couldn't disagree.

Snapping her book shut, she glared back at Abel.

"Leave me alone!" she yelled. "Stop following me around and staring at me! You're driving me nuts!"

"I don't know what you're talking about. Seems like you have an anger problem," Abel said, sauntering over to the patio. "Maybe you should get that looked at by a professional."

Her whole body shook with the effort it took not to jump at him. "Is that scar of yours getting worse, or are you just getting uglier?"

His smile vanished.

"Too bad a nice lady like Gwyneth has such a horrible niece. I bet her life would be much better without someone like you in it."

Abel walked away from her before she could reply.

He smelled like silver.

Nine

Secrets

Seth was surprised to find his brother at home when he returned from school the next day. Abel had been practically living at Rylie's ranch for the last week while Eleanor did research, leaving Seth a lot of time alone at home.

"Where's Mom?" Seth asked, dropping his backpack on a clear patch of floor. Everywhere else was covered in boxes and news articles. They only had one piece of furniture—a table given to them by a family down the street—and even that was plastered with notes.

Abel stretched, reaching his hands for the ceiling. "She's at the library again. Feel like having a skirmish?"

Seth had a lot of homework to do, but he and his brother hadn't had a good practice fight since he got the cast off. "Sure."

They moved to the empty yard outside. With the fence at their backs and the nearest mobile homes empty, they had almost total privacy. Seth stripped off his shirt so it wouldn't get sweaty.

"You're home late," Abel remarked as he put on a pair of gloves with padded knuckles. They usually fought barehanded, but Seth couldn't show up to school with black eyes, so they started using protection.

"I had a track meet."

Abel laughed. "Seriously?"

"Seriously."

His brother swung at him, and Seth dodged easily. It was a slow move meant to start the fight rather than actually hit him. He twisted under it and jabbed his elbow at Abel.

"What's next? Football and dating some cheerleader?"

"Maybe," Seth said.

Abel caught his fist and used it to throw him against the tree. "I never thought you'd get into this stupid teenager stuff. You want to be prom king or something?"

"I *am* a teenager." His fist sunk into Abel's gut, but his brother turned at just the right time to send it sliding off his ribs. "What are you doing at home anyway? I thought you were working a hundred hours a week at your new job."

"The old lady insisted I take a day off. Who am I to argue? I've been missing my little brother."

Abel swung an uppercut that snapped Seth's head back. The yard flashed with black stars.

He held up a hand to ask for a pause, working his jaw to clear the ringing in his skull. He should have been able to escape that one. His leg was still slowing him down. Abel stood back, fists waiting.

"So now you're spying on me for Mom? Is that what this is?"

To his credit, Abel looked offended. "I just want to know what you're up to." He didn't need to say that Eleanor didn't really care what Seth was doing between the new and full moons anyway. They both knew it, and the knowledge stung.

Taking a few deep breaths to center himself, Seth nodded.

They exchanged blows silently except for the occasional grunt and the meaty sound of fist hitting flesh. He gave as good as he got. Even though Abel was almost twice his size, he was fast, and he thought he might have gotten better since his solo hunt over the summer.

But Seth's calf muscle kept locking up, and Abel knocked him to the dirt more than once.

After getting flattened for the third time, he held up a hand to stop him again. Abel gripped his wrist and hauled him to his feet. "Shake it off, man."

"Yeah. Right." All of Seth's running at school was slowing down his recovery. It was easy to forget that most people would have still been in a cast so soon after the injury. Even someone with his speedy healing should have taken a break occasionally.

But most people weren't from a family of hunters. Abel and Eleanor weren't going to give him a break for long.

"How's school?" Abel asked, giving Seth a little space as he rubbed hard at his calf. He almost made it sound like he cared.

"It's fine."

It was torture seeing Rylie hanging out with other guys, though. It made him feel even more beaten than he did after a fight with Abel. But his brother wouldn't have wanted to hear that.

"Nobody giving you trouble for being new?"

"Nah. What kind of stuff have you been doing at the Gresham ranch?"

Abel's eyes lit up. Now they were talking about something he was actually interested in. "Working." He didn't mean he was working a job—he meant he was hunting. "I'm getting close, bro."

Seth swallowed hard. His fists dropped a little.

"Who?" he asked, voice hoarse.

"At first I thought it was one of the ranch hands. Migrant workers, you know? There's been that upswing of attacks in Central America. But the guys are clean. The one in the hospital is healing at a normal speed, and the other one is as much a werewolf as I am a fairy." Abel bounced from foot to foot, shadow boxing with an invisible enemy. "It's the girl. That kid. I'm almost sure."

Seth dropped his guard. Abel's fist connected with the side of his head.

The world exploded into black stars. He went down, hitting the dirt with a thud that jarred his recently healed leg. His elbow banged against a rock.

"Hey!"

"Hey yourself. What's wrong with you? Why aren't you paying attention?"

He cradled his ringing skull and grimaced at his brother. Abel had dropped all pretense of a fight. "She's kind of young for a werewolf. Teens almost never survive the attacks."

"Her aunt said Rylie has been getting into trouble at school. And the way she stares at me..." Abel shook his head. "Her eyes are that gold color in the sunlight. It's a dead giveaway."

He offered Seth a hand to pull him up again, but he didn't take it.

"You can't tell Mom."

Abel laughed, but it died off when he saw that Seth wasn't laughing too. "You're serious." His gaze sharpened. "Did you already know?"

"Abel..."

"How did you find out? Why the hell didn't you tell us?"

Seth dusted off his jeans as he stood. "It's complicated."

"Complicated? Are you hot for her or something?" The question was half-joking, but when Seth didn't respond, tension rippled through Abel. He wasn't smiling at all anymore. "She's a werewolf."

"Rylie is different."

"Different? *Different?*"

He was starting to get loud. Seth kept an eye on the street, holding his hands out to soothe him. If Eleanor chose that moment to come home, Rylie would be done for. "Quiet down, man. I can explain. I've known for awhile, okay? She's my... friend."

Abel stared at him in stony silence. There were gold flecks in his eyes much like Rylie's. Even though he had never become a wolf, he looked more animal than she ever had.

Seth wasn't afraid of his brother like other people were. They watched each other's backs. He would have given his life for Abel a hundred times if he could have. But that look was terrifying, and he had to swallow hard to keep the bile from rising in his throat.

"This summer," Abel said finally, carefully enunciating every word as if to make absolutely sure Seth understood him. "You didn't kill the wolf at Camp Golden Lake, did you?"

"The werewolf is dead, but that's kind of why it's complicated. I didn't kill him. Rylie did it."

He folded his arms. They were so muscular that they couldn't lay flat on his chest. "Sounds like you've got a lot to tell me."

"Yeah. I'll tell you everything." Two trailers down, someone hauled a bag of charcoal out to their barbecue, and Seth lowered his voice. "But not here. Can we go for a walk?"

His brother nodded stiffly.

They left the mobile home community, walking along the side of the empty road away from town. His sweat made the wind feel chillier, so Seth patted his chest and underarms dry with his shirt. Thunder rolled in the distance. "Well?" Abel demanded.

Seth pulled his shirt over his head and smoothed down his hair to give himself time to think. "The werewolf at camp was trying to make a pack. He'd already turned one other girl before he bit Rylie. I tried to save her. I wasn't fast enough."

"So what? You feel responsible for her?"

"Well, I just thought I could help her. You didn't change when you were bitten. But... on the last moon, the other werewolf almost got me. So Rylie chose to change. She wanted to save me." Seth stopped to face Abel. "She changed for *me*."

Abel's expression froze. "They lose their souls after they transform. She's not the girl you knew."

"But she's *different*," Seth insisted. "She had a chance to kill me after she changed, but she walked away. My leg was a wreck. I couldn't have fought her. Have you ever seen a werewolf walk away from easy prey?"

"No, but a werewolf under control wouldn't eat living cows, either."

"You would do it if they held still long enough." Seth tried to make himself smile, but he couldn't put any feeling into it. "You can't tell Mom. She'll blow her lid."

"Are you going to feel this way when she starts eating people? Do you want to be responsible for those lives?" he asked.

"She won't do it. I'm serious, Abel."

"I am too! I've been studying up on your little girlfriend. Did you know she got into a fight on her first day at school here? And she attacked a ranch hand with a shovel."

"She has it under control," Seth said stubbornly.

They stared each other down while the wind blew and the sun slowly set. He would have given a lot of money to know what Abel was thinking.

"Come on, bro," he finally said. "A werewolf? At least cheerleaders aren't going to rip out your throat when you take them on a date."

"You only think that because you never went to high school. Promise, Abel. Promise me you won't tell Mom."

He could tell he won as soon as Abel's gaze dropped.

"Fine." He held up a finger. "But I'm not going to lie if she asks me, and when she goes out to hunt on the new moon, I'm going to go with her. And you have to stay away from Rylie."

Seth nodded reluctantly. It was the best he could ask for. Abel stalked back to the trailer park, leaving his brother alone.

Ten

The Process

Abel showed up at the ranch late on Friday. When he finally arrived, he didn't even look at Rylie even though he passed right by her. He immediately joined Jorge in the fields and got to work.

She climbed to a ridge overlooking the fields, shaded by the half-bare branches of a tree, and watched him walk through the pasture. Having him ignore her didn't make her feel any better. Instead, she wondered what he was planning to do next.

Rylie couldn't stand to watch. She went inside the house.

The smell of nutmeg and ginger wafted through the air. Gwyn was using butternut squash and the last of their eggs to bake pies. There was already one in the oven and another cooling on the counter.

Her aunt was hunched over her barstool, slowly rolling out the dough for the next pie. She looked terrible.

Rylie felt a tremor of worry. Gwyn never sat inside for long. "What are you doing?"

"Wash your hands," she ordered. She may have looked bad, but she sounded just as authoritative as ever. "You know, your dad made great pumpkin pies when we were kids. Nobody made crusts better than Brian. They came out even flakier than your grandma's."

"He said the secret was ice water and careful math." The thought of her dad's smiling face gave Rylie chest pangs. "Pie was the only thing he could make... and extra crispy bacon." Her voice caught on the last word. She swiped at her eyes with the towel while she dried her hands, hoping Gwyn wouldn't nice.

"I could sure use Brian's magic for these pies. Why don't you make the next batch of dough?"

Rylie pulled on an old apron to protect her denim skirt from flour. "You didn't come to his funeral," she said, trying to make it sound casual. A tear plopped on the counter.

Gwyn sighed and set down the rolling pin. "I'm sorry, babe. I've been waiting for you to ask about that."

"Why?"

"It's hard to explain. You gotta trust me when I say I wouldn't have missed it if it wasn't for a real good reason."

"My mom told me that it was because you were busy selling your old ranch and forgot," Rylie said. "She thinks you've always liked your work better than your family."

"Jessica doesn't know anything about me." Gwyn's voice slashed through the kitchen. "Got that?"

She gave a sullen nod to the bag of flour. "Then why?"

"I'm not ready to tell you."

Rylie chewed on her lip as she retrieved ice from the freezer, setting it in a half-filled bowl of water. She knew she should leave it alone, but the questions were bursting inside of her, and she didn't know how to keep quiet.

"Was it a new girlfriend?" she asked, setting the bowl down. "Were you fighting with my dad? Was it—"

Gwyn smacked her hand on the kitchen island to silence her.

"Shut up. You don't know what you're asking."

"I can't know unless you tell me," she said.

"I love you, kid, and I love your dad, but it's none of your business. Got it?"

Rylie forced herself to shut her mouth. Her aunt's cold blue eyes lit up with fire, and that expression left no room for argument. The threat of getting sent back to the city hovered between them. She couldn't forget she was only at her aunt's as a favor.

She changed the subject. "So why did you say you're not working outside with the guys?"

"I didn't. The men are doing fine on their own." Gwyn laid the crust in a glass pie dish and pressed down the edges with a fork. She shot her niece a sideways look. "Is that Abel bothering you? I'll get rid of him if you want."

The offer surprised Rylie. She hadn't expected Gwyn to notice the tension, much less care enough to fire Abel. There was too much work to be done before the winter. It was tempting, though, and Rylie kneaded the dough as she considered it.

The wolf didn't want him to go. The wolf liked having Abel where they could watch him.

"I don't know," Rylie said, and she was surprised when the words came out in a half-growl like it did before she changed on the full moon. She coughed to clear her throat. "I thought you were his number one fan. You've practically written poetry about him."

"I'm nobody's number one fan but yours," Gwyn said. She managed to make even that compliment sound half-insulting. "Give it some thought. Say the word and he's gone."

She slopped the pie mix into the dish, and they shared a smile. Rylie's was much toothier than her aunt's.

Once the remaining pies were cooking, Rylie went down to the pond and sat on a bench the last owner's had left behind. It was covered in ivy. She plucked at the brown leaves as she mulled over the idea of firing Abel. Seth's brother terrified her. It would be much safer to keep him away.

But what if he found out that Rylie asked for him to get fired? Would that be the last piece of the puzzle he needed to confirm that she was the werewolf?

Jorge and Abel went into the house to talk to Gwyn, kicking the mud off their boots by the front door. They were gone for several minutes. Rylie kicked at her little pile of shredded leaves, pushing it into the edge of the pond.

When the men left again, Jorge went to his car and Abel came to stand in front of Rylie's bench.

"I know the truth about you," he said in a low voice.

She leapt to her feet, baring her teeth. She might have gone for his throat if the back door hadn't opened again.

"Rylie!" Gwyn called.

Thick cords of muscle stood out on Abel's neck. Tension shivered between them.

"Well?" Rylie whispered.

She wanted him to attack her. She wanted an excuse to kill him. The wolf envisioned reopening his old wounds and finishing the job, and it could almost taste the blood.

Could she turn Abel if she bit him again? Could he be her pack? Or would she have to eat him piece by piece?

"Rylie!"

"Stay the hell away from my brother," Abel hissed.

She stared after him as he jogged to his motorcycle and roared away. It was all she could do not to chase him. Her thoughts were buzzing around in her skull too fast to process.

"I'm not calling your name again!" Gwyn shouted, and the screen door slammed shut.

Her knees wobbled, so she sat back down on the bench. The wolf faded away, leaving nothing inside of her but the shivering embers of fear.

He knew.

And the next moon was only three days away.

•○•

Seth walked home alone. Abel had told him to come back as soon as he finished school, but he wasted time exploring instead, wandering through the streets with no destination in mind. Everything in town was close enough to reach on foot—the west edge was only three miles from the east edge, and their community was a half mile past that.

He fantasized about his mom getting angry at him for disappearing. She could ground him. No TV or games for the week. The idea of it made him laugh.

By the time he got to their mobile home, it was getting dark. Their trailer was in the position his mom considered to be best for defense, and he didn't make eye contact with anybody living around them to make sure he remained detached. If he started to like people, he might want to stay—and that wasn't an option.

Abel pulled weeds in the yard without a shirt. It used to be that women flocked to gaze at him, but now that he was scarred, everyone watched from an uneasy distance as if they were afraid he would attack.

He wasn't trying to make the trailer look better. Seth knew that. It was part of his ongoing physical conditioning. Just one more thing to make him stronger and harder.

"Done wasting time for the day?" Abel called when Seth approached. Four silvery, parallel scars striped his ribs down to the navel. It was a permanent souvenir of the night he had been bitten by a werewolf.

"Done stalking the Greshams for the day?" Seth snapped back.

"Nope. I'm pulling a double shift today. The old lady insisted I go home for dinner, but I'm going back to repair the tractor tonight so we can use it tomorrow."

His voice sounded funny. Seth lowered his voice. "You didn't do anything weird, did you?"

"No." Abel stuffed a fistful of foxtails in a trash bag. "But I should have."

"We don't kill humans," he whispered.

His brother's eyes glowed like he was considering making an exception.

Eleanor sat on the floor inside their trailer, surrounded by newspaper clippings. A small stack of banker's boxes stood against the wall. She was in the middle of what she called *the process*. She would sift through crime reports, write headlines in her notebook, and rank how likely she thought they were to be related to the werewolf.

The only decoration on their wall was a map of the region printed onto several pages. This was part of the process, too. Once she picked the most likely werewolf articles, she would stab color-coded pins into the map to mark where they occurred.

Piece by piece, Eleanor would mark the werewolf's territory. She would use that map to find its den.

And then, on the next moon, they would kill it.

His mom looked like a snake coiled in the middle of the room waiting for someone to wander close enough to strike. She had been born in the wrong era. She was meant to be Boadicea or Wu Zetian—a queen conquering the old world. Eleanor was beautiful and smart and ruthless. She had killed a dozen werewolves on her own.

One red pin marked the map on the wall. It was centered over Rylie's ranch.

"Found anything yet?" he asked.

Eleanor responded by pointing at the boxes. "I'm looking at domestic violence cases. Help me sort."

"I've got a lot of homework to do."

"Did I ask you if you have homework? No. I told you to help me sort. Sit down."

He dropped his backpack and did what she ordered, making sure not to disturb her piles. "Why domestic violence?"

"I got no other leads yet, so I'm working with the basics. Werewolves are often batterers," Eleanor said by rote.

Her husband—Seth and Abel's father—was considered the expert on werewolves by most hunters. He had literally written the book on tracking and killing them, and he used to make everyone in the family recite passages until they had them memorized.

Eleanor hadn't stopped studying his work after he was killed.

"What are we going to do for dinner?" Seth asked, separating the articles into two random piles. There wasn't much point in reading them when he knew Rylie wasn't a wife beater.

His mom glanced at her watch, looking surprised to realize it was getting late. "I don't know, and I don't have time to worry about it. There are leftover tacos in the fridge." They had been eating fast food for every meal since they arrived in town.

Before Seth could say something else, Eleanor had refocused on the task at hand. She hadn't wondered, even for a moment, why he was so late coming home. He wasn't sure she even realized he was still going to school.

He stared at the red pin on the Gresham ranch.

Rylie's aunt would notice if she was out late.

"How long do you think this will take?" Seth asked.

"Not long." She finally gave him a smile. "Not long at all."

He pretended to sort articles for an hour, but when Abel left to go back to the ranch, Seth left too. Eleanor didn't ask where he was going. She always hoped he would come back with something dead when he ducked out, like a good werewolf hunter should. Or maybe she just didn't care.

He found himself outside Rylie's house a half hour later. Abel's motorcycle was parked outside the barn, and the lights were on inside. He avoided his brother and went up the hill to the house instead.

Seth watched Rylie and her aunt have dinner through the window. They were sharing beef ribs drenched in barbecue sauce, and the two of them sat close together at the table, smiling when they talked and looking happier than he could ever remember being with his own family.

Anybody else might have thought they were completely normal—anyone who wasn't a hunter. But Seth could sense Rylie the way he could smell trash rotting in a dumpster. All werewolves felt like that to him.

The way she moved and looked at her aunt wasn't normal, either. She didn't look like she belonged in a house, a city, or anywhere near other humans.

A rib bone almost fell off the table, and Gwyneth made a sudden motion to catch it. Rylie jerked. It was a small gesture, but she had to shut her eyes and take deep breaths before she could go back to what she was doing.

Her prey drive had kicked in at the fast motion. Seth had seen it too many times before.

Rylie was different from other werewolves. Seth believed it. He really did. But she was still dangerous. If his family didn't get her, then it might be some other hunter putting a bullet in her skull someday. He had done it himself before. He could imagine the way Rylie's blood would spray all too clearly.

He waited outside until they finished dinner and Gwyneth went to bed. Rylie washed dishes in the sink by the open window.

The wind shifted. Her head lifted, and she looked right through the shadows to where he stood.

Seth tried to duck down the hill, but it was too late. Rylie stormed out the back door. "This isn't camp anymore," she said. "You can't lurk outside my house."

"Come on, Rylie, I just want to—"

He only had an instant to dodge. Rylie flung a cast-iron skillet at his head, and it smashed into the bushes behind him. "Go away!"

"I came back because I want to help you!"

She moved to throw a soapy sponge, but his words made her hand freeze in the middle of the motion. "You want to help? How?"

"My mom's not onto you yet," Seth said, "but she's working on it. She'll figure it out soon."

"You told Abel about me, didn't you?"

"No. Well, yeah. But he already knew." He could tell he was losing her. Rylie started moving back toward the house—probably to find another heavy projectile. "I want to help you hide on the next moon."

That stopped her. "Why?"

"I don't want you to die, Rylie."

"Oh."

"I want to apologize, too," he said. "I don't have any right to tell you to leave."

Her anger sparked again, even hotter than before. She stalked toward him. "You need to leave me alone. I'm a monster, aren't I? You don't want to make me angry!"

"Do you think you could beat me?" Seth asked.

"Maybe I could!"

"Do you think you could beat my brother? My mom? How about both of them at the same time?"

Her eyes flashed. "Is that a threat?"

"No." Seth took a deep breath. "My family is good. Really good. You're going to get caught one of these nights. There's no way you can avoid them without my help."

"You said it would be better for us to avoid each other. What changed your mind?"

It was a good question. His mom would kill him if she found out he was helping a werewolf. It was why he hadn't told them the truth about the summer when he came home. Seth couldn't tell Rylie that—she wouldn't understand.

"I tried to save you on the night you were bitten. I failed, and I've been paying for it ever since."

It was the wrong thing to say. Her fists clenched. "So I'm a punishment?"

"No, but I can still save you." He spoke fast. "We're going to get the beast under control so you can hide until my family thinks you've moved on. Then we'll leave. You can stay."

Seth watched the werewolf's fury drain out of her, leaving normal, harmless Rylie in its wake. She nudged a weed with her toe. Her feet were bare. "Okay," she said. Rylie peeked at him through her hair, and she finally smiled a little. "You want to come inside and talk? We have leftovers."

He shook his head. "I should get back to my mom. She'll wonder where I am." It was a lie, but Seth didn't want to sit in a house where people loved each other and be unable to share in it. "We'll talk at school when Abel isn't watching. At least we know he'll be here most of the time. He's good, but he can't be everywhere at once."

"And what about your mom?"

"Yeah, Seth. What about Mom?"

Abel emerged from the shadows. Seth moved to stand in front of Rylie even though he had already seen them.

"You're supposed to be working on the tractor," Seth said.

"Yeah, but then I saw our car, and I wondered why you were visiting the ranch. I didn't think you would be visiting the *werewolf*." He spat out the last word, and Rylie tensed behind Seth. Her hands gripped his arm. "I thought I told you to stay away."

"I came here to see her," Seth said. "She didn't want to see me. It's not her fault."

Abel clenched his jaw. His hands hovered near his back, where he usually kept a handgun. Seth was armed, too—but his gun was strapped to his ankle. He wondered if he could draw faster than his brother.

Rylie radiated tension behind Seth. It was like having an attack dog leaning against his legs.

"Relax," Seth muttered.

Abel's eyes dropped to the place that Rylie touched Seth, and anger flashed across his face. He grabbed Seth by the back of the shirt and threw him across the hill.

Pain flared up his leg, and Seth slammed to the dirt.

Rylie took a step toward him, but Abel jabbed a finger in her chest to stop her. "I won't warn you again. Stay away from him." He faced his brother. "Get in the car. If you don't go home right now, I'll tell Mom where you've been."

Seth tried to catch Rylie's eye, but she wasn't looking at him. Her gaze was fixed on Abel. It was such a dark night that she was a silhouette against the sky, but her pupils reflected the light of the moon. She looked bestial. The hair rose on the back of Seth's arms.

She didn't move when Seth drove down the hill with Abel's motorcycle right behind him, but by the time he turned the corner, she had vanished.

Eleven

The Bite

Seth and Rylie didn't talk openly at school. Even though she didn't see Abel circling the school in his Chevelle anymore, neither of them wanted to tempt fate.

They slipped each other notes as they passed in the hallways. Rylie wished she could have told him what she was really thinking in her letters, but they kept it strictly business. The new moon was coming in two days. They needed a plan.

She sat with Tate and his dumb friends like usual over those two days, picking at her roast beef with less enthusiasm than usual. Seth was eating with a bunch of jocks on the other side of the quad. He had joined the track team like the rumors said, and now it looked like they were trying to recruit him for football, too. In such a small school, most athletes played all the sports.

Rylie would have preferred to sit with him instead of listening to the guys talk about video games and weed. And judging by the occasional looks Seth threw in her direction, he didn't like her sitting with them very much, either.

The day before the new moon came too soon. The sun was setting earlier in the day, and she struggled with control as it got darker. Rylie couldn't sit with Gwyn that night. She begged sick and hid in her room to watch the minutes tick by on the clock instead.

If she closed her eyes and took deep breaths, she could almost smell the faint odors of pine and icy river water. It was like Gray Mountain had followed her out into the country, and the wolf longed to run through the forest.

The distant rumble of a motorcycle's engine approached. She stood by her bay window, suspended in fear as she peered through the dark night. Was it Seth or Abel coming up her road?

The wind shifted and she caught a smell of the rider.

Seth.

She peeked into the hallway one last time to make sure her aunt's bedroom light was out before slipping out her window and running to him.

"Get on," he said, tossing his helmet to her.

"Why do I have to wear it and you don't?"

"Because I only have one helmet. Hurry up. We don't have much time."

Rylie tugged it on over her head, hoping it wouldn't give her funny hair. She had spent ages in front of the mirror with the flat iron and makeup even though she always woke up after a moon looking like she had been caught in a stampede.

Sliding her arms around Seth's waist, she rested her head against his broad back with a sigh. He felt even more solid than he looked. She was glad the motorcycle drowned out the sound of her smelling his back.

They rushed through the night with the wind beating around them. Seth must have been going way over the speed limit, but the roads were empty, and nobody tried to stop them.

He stopped a good thirty miles north of town, and Rylie got off, smoothing her hair self-consciously as Seth hid the motorcycle in a cluster of bushes.

"Where are we?" she asked.

"You'll see," he said. "Follow me."

They hiked across the empty hill. It might have been nice getting to walk alone with Seth if she hadn't been feeling so moon-sick. Thousands of stars were visible this far from the city, and Rylie thoughts he could see a misty galaxy stretching above the horizon.

But the sky wasn't half as interesting as sneaking a peek at Seth. He had a little bit of beard growth on the sides of his jaw, and it made him look older. Rylie didn't think he had any stubble when they kissed over the summer, but it had been so fast, it was hard to tell. He'd grabbed her while the other werewolves were attacking the camp, and she'd barely had time to realize what was happening, much less enjoy it.

Rylie wondered what a beard would feel like against her cheek. Did he still like her like that? What if she tried to kiss him again?

"What are you looking at?" Seth asked.

She blushed. "Nothing."

"Do you feel like you're going to change soon?"

All business. Of course. "No, not yet. I still have a few minutes," she said. Seth looked up at the wrong part of the sky, searching for the new moon. Rylie found it hard to believe that he didn't know where it was when she could feel it pulling at her with silver hooks.

"Good, because we still have a few minutes of walking. Don't change and eat me yet." He smiled when he said it, but Rylie didn't laugh. "What's wrong?"

"I'm worried about your family," she admitted. "Knowing someone out there wants to kill me is scary."

"I'm sorry," Seth said.

"Have you tried telling them you don't want to be a hunter? They would probably understand. Everyone's parents want them to go to college and stuff."

He shook his head. "I can't do that. Abel might have been able to if he wanted, but he's not like me and Dad. Mom and

Abel are hunters. Not kopes." She stared at him blankly.
"Don't ask. It's stupid."

"No, you have to tell me now. What is that?"

"It's like... I don't know, being destined to hunt stuff. It's
not magic, but I'm stronger than most people, and a little faster
and I can... okay, this sounds really stupid. Don't laugh. I can
sense werewolves."

Rylie's eyes widened. "You can *sense* me? Like Spiderman?"

"I said it was stupid," Seth said, swinging his backpack into
a bush as they passed it.

"No. That's cool. So you're weird, like me."

"I was born into it, not bitten."

"But you're still not normal," she insisted.

"I guess. So that's why Mom thinks I should be a great hunter,
like Dad was before he died. Killing werewolves was his specialty.
I guess I'm good at it too, but who wants to do that? It's not like a
career."

"You don't want to do it because you're a good person.
You're better than them."

The subject obviously made him uncomfortable. He
shrugged. "Whatever."

"So what does that word mean?" Rylie asked. "'Kopes'?
Who made that up?"

"I don't know. It's Greek or something."

"Oh."

They walked on quietly, footsteps whispering in the dry
grass. Rylie moved a lot faster than Seth did, even on flat
ground, and she had to make herself slow down so she
wouldn't lose him in the night.

The sparse trees grew a little closer together, and they made
their way around a dense thicket.

"What else can you do?" Rylie asked. "Can you dodge
bullets?"

He laughed. "No. That's pretty much it. I can bench press
at least three hundred pounds, though, and I don't work out

much. Abel used to get annoyed about it, but he's a lot stronger now that he got bitten."

"I wonder how much I can lift," she said. "You know, since I'm a werewolf. I've never even tried." Some of her guy friends back home had been into weightlifting. They talked about their veins and doing lots of reps to get big biceps, and it was just about the most boring thing she could imagine.

"I don't think wolves can bench press anything with their paws," Seth said, grinning. Rylie rolled her eyes.

They finally came across an area that had been leveled off. A concrete path was laid out into the side of the hill, and a tunnel led into a big padlocked door with boards nailed over it. They had to climb over a fence to get there, but despite all the NO TRESPASSING signs, there wasn't any security.

Seth found a big rock and struck the padlock on the door. It snapped off. Rylie peeked at a worn map by the door, and was surprised to see they were standing over a mine.

"A mine?" she asked doubtfully while Seth pried off the boards. "Aren't those kind of dangerous?"

"You got a better idea?"

"Dungeon? Cliffside cave? Outer space?"

He laughed. "I'll build a space station for your next moon. This is all we have tonight."

The wood splintered and fractured. Seth flung it aside and shoved the door, but it only slid open an inch. She kept an eye on the empty plains around them as he struggled.

The night was so clear that she could have seen a coyote approaching from miles away. A human hunter would have been even more obvious. Even though she could tell they were completely alone, Rylie still felt like she was being watched, and she wanted to get somewhere sheltered.

Seth backed up to stand beside her, wiping the sweat off his upper lip.

"Is something wrong?" she asked.

"This is a gold mine. The price of gold has to be really high to make a profit off its operations, so they shut it down the rest of the time. It's not running now. I think they put something against the back of the door. I can't open it."

"Some super strong hunter guy you are. Let me try."

Rylie took his place and shoved against the door. It groaned open. She barely had to strain.

Seth stared. "You didn't seriously just do that."

"I bet I can bench press a million pounds," she said. "How much did you say you can do? Three hundred pounds? That's awesome, Seth. Good job. I'm super impressed."

He shoved her playfully. "Shut up and get inside."

Seth took a flashlight out of his backpack and pointed it inside. The mine was nothing like Rylie expected. Everything was built of smooth concrete, and the cool, dark air was dry on her skin. Seth illuminated their path as they descended a long flight of steps twisting around an elevator shaft.

"It's so dark," Rylie whispered. "Are there lights?"

"Yeah, but they've cut the power."

She shivered. "I don't think I want to change in here."

"I'll leave a lantern for you," Seth said. "I've got one in my backpack."

"It's scary."

"You're going to be a lot scarier in less than an hour." He checked his watch. "More like twenty minutes. Let's hurry."

They explored until they reached an unlocked room. Rylie didn't know what it had been used for, but it was empty now, and it had a metal door like it was a giant safe. Seth turned on the lantern and set it in the corner.

"I guess this will work," she said. "Where will you be?"

"I'm going to leave the mine and shut the surface door in case you get out. You can't hurt anything in the mine, so don't worry about it." He pulled a bundle of black straps out of his bag. "I have some ropes and a muzzle if you want. Just like old times."

She had to laugh. "This is kind of funny, huh? It's like summer all over again. Except..." Except this time, she was really turning into a werewolf.

"Summer wasn't all that funny," Seth said, his smile fading.

"No. It wasn't." Rylie curled a lock of blond hair around her finger. "I was worried about you. I missed you."

He touched her arm. "Yeah. I missed you too."

"I don't want to wear the muzzle."

Seth threw it in the bag again. "I'll see you in the morning."

Rylie nodded without speaking. There was nothing left to say.

The door made a heavy *clang* when he shut it. Rylie knelt by the lantern, staring into the bulb until her eyes burned and she blinked green spots. It was so dark in the mine that it felt like the shadows had substance and closed around her like thick folds of velvet.

The tug of the moon wasn't as persistent underground. Rylie almost thought it wouldn't be able to reach her and that she wouldn't have to change.

Almost.

•○•

Seth fought to shove the door shut once he reached the surface, but it was much harder without Rylie's help. No matter how he pushed and pulled and strained at it, he couldn't make it budge.

The timer on his watch beeped. It was time.

He glanced up at the sky, wishing he had Abel's ability to sense the motion of the new moon. Would Rylie be starting to change, or had she already become the werewolf and begun moving toward him?

He didn't want to find out. He groaned as he threw his weight into the door, squeezing his eyes shut and digging his heels into the dirt.

"What are you doing?"

Seth froze. He knew that voice.

He muttered a silent prayer before turning around.

"Hi, Mom," he said.

If Eleanor was frightening in the middle of her process, she was a complete nightmare on a moon. She stood four inches taller than him in combat boots with her hair pulled into a knot that made her face look like it was blown back by the wind. The rifle in her hands suited her like another appendage. Silver ammo hung from her belt.

And the look she gave Seth dripped with suspicion.

Abel loomed behind her. His broad-shouldered form would have been easy to mistake for a bear.

He realized she was waiting for him to answer her question. "Hunting," Seth said. "I'm... hunting." He moved his body to block the crack in the door, trying to discreetly shift his weight against it, but it was still stuck. "What are you doing here?"

His explanation seemed to satisfy Eleanor. She noted his lack of weapons and drew a pistol from her thigh holster, handing it to Seth. He checked the cartridge. It was loaded with homemade silver bullets, too.

"We're hunting too. Abel's been tracking the wolf's smell. He picked it up at the Gresham farm."

Seth looked over in time to see Abel slip a gray box into his pocket. He felt like he had been punched in the stomach. It was his brother's GPS receiver, which let him track the anti-theft devices he'd installed on his motorcycle and Chevelle. He hadn't sniffed out Rylie. He had known Seth would go see her and followed them to her hideout.

"Good sense of smell," Seth said.

Abel met his gaze without blinking. "Good thing we got here in time. You could have been hurt."

Eleanor didn't notice the silent conversation passing between her sons. She pushed Seth aside to look in the mine. "What's this? Is that where it's hiding?"

"I thought it might be a good place for the werewolf to use as a den, but I didn't find anything. I was closing it up so I wouldn't get caught trespassing."

Abel knew him too well. His eyes sharpened. "Let's take another look."

"No!"

Eleanor arched an eyebrow. "No?"

"Uh…" He thought fast. "It's condemned."

"I'm disappointed, Seth. A werewolf would have no interest in a mine. There's not enough prey. Let's get out of here before we're found," she said, and Abel looked like he was on the verge of exploding.

"Mom—" he began.

And then a noise echoed from the mine.

It wasn't much of a noise. They probably wouldn't have even noticed it under normal circumstances. It was a distant dragging sound, like hauling a heavy sack across the cement, and it faded within a second.

But it was one sound too many from an abandoned mine.

Eleanor and Abel exchanged looks.

"Shut the door," Seth said as a second dragging sound echoed form the earth. He didn't have to see what was happening to imagine a bloody, newly-changed werewolf pulling herself up the stairs. It wouldn't be Rylie down there. It would be something else entirely. "Shut the door!"

"Why—?"

"Just do it!"

His mom looked surprised enough by his change in attitude that she didn't stop him when he shoved her aside and grabbed the handle, hauling with all his strength.

The sliding changed to the padding sound of paws, and then a growl.

A very close growl.

Seth pulled one more time, but it was too late. White fur flashed in the darkness. Eleanor lifted her rifle.

And then Rylie leaped out of the mine.

A huge, furred body struck him, and his leg gave out. He hit the ground. The pistol skittered out of his hand.

"Shoot it!" Eleanor shouted.

He had never seen a werewolf move as fast as Rylie. She was a white-gold blur darting through the night. She snarled and snapped at Abel, who jammed his rifle in her mouth just in time to keep her jaws from closing on his face.

Throwing her to the ground, he tried to bring his gun to bear, but Rylie jumped at him again before he could collect himself.

Black blood cascaded down his shoulder as she ripped free of him. Shreds of his skin dangled between her teeth. Abel roared and collapsed.

"Stop!" Seth yelled.

She crouched over Abel and glared at him. Her gold eyes were like twin full moons. Did she recognize him? He couldn't tell, and he wasn't willing to bet on it enough to make a move for his brother.

Eleanor turned at an angle to get the wolf in her sights without endangering Abel.

Rylie burst into motion when she fired.

For a terrifying motion, he was sure she had been hit. But when Rylie landed, she shifted direction and bounded toward the fence, scaling it in an instant.

She rushed into the hills beyond, completely unfazed. Eleanor must have missed.

Spinning, Seth's mom fired a half dozen shots into the darkness, but Rylie was already gone. "Dammit!" she swore, punching a fist into the air.

Seth scrambled to Abel's side. He was curled into a ball and his face twisted with pain. Pushing him onto his back, Seth found his brother's skin sweaty and ashen. Abel had his hands jammed against the wound, and he could almost fit his entire fist in it.

With a chill, Seth recalled that horrible night when his brother had first been bitten by a werewolf. What would a second bite do to him?

"Stay with Abel," Eleanor commanded. "I'm going after that thing."

"I don't think I can get him home alone, Mom," he called. When she didn't turn, he got to his feet. "Mom!"

She slung her rifle over her shoulder and scaled the fence.

Seth was torn. Abel was bleeding and groaning on the ground. He might be fine—but he also might not. Rylie was out there with Eleanor, and he wasn't sure who he would bet on if they came face to face again.

He couldn't face Abel alone. Praying that Rylie's speed was greater than his mom's wits, Seth hauled his brother to his feet.

"Let's get you home."

Twelve

Golden Hair

"Ouch! Watch it!"

"Shut up and stop being a sissy," Seth said.

Abel sat on the kitchen counter, hunched forward so his head wouldn't bump the cabinets. The family first aid kit was open on their kitchen table and the bottle of painkillers had been tipped to spill pills across the surface. Abel had swallowed a handful of them as soon as they got home. Now he was high enough to withstand Seth's sloppiest attempts at stitching him up.

Biting his tongue, Seth moved slowly with his needle and wire to stitch the injury. There wasn't a lot he could do. Rylie had bitten deep and it would definitely scar.

"Sissy? You think I'm a sissy? You're not the one who got eaten by a werewolf!"

Seth's hand slipped. Abel grunted. "Sorry." He cut the wire on the right side and knotted it, leaving five sloppy stitches, and went to work on the other side.

"You owe me thanks, bro. You could have been bitten if we hadn't been there."

"Rylie would never attack me."

"You sure?"

"Yes," he said. The more he thought about the moment his eyes met Rylie's, the more sure he was that she recognized him. Any other werewolf would have attacked him too. Most of them were mindless animals, but she wasn't.

"She would have come out of that mine and—ow!" Abel shoved Seth away from him. "Give me the needle. I'll do it myself."

"You've taken so many drugs that you couldn't legally operate a pair of safety scissors. I'm not giving you a needle."

"At least I don't have the sewing skill of a Mack truck."

Seth jabbed his elbow into Abel's side when he tried to grab the needle again. Normally, his brother wouldn't have put up with that kind of treatment, but the painkillers made him sluggish.

"I told you to shut up."

"What was I saying?" Abel asked, swaying where he sat. "Oh yeah. Your girlfriend would have come out of that mine and killed you if we hadn't been there. You weren't even armed. You think the power of *love* is going to save you? Is love made of silver alloy?"

"She's not my girlfriend," Seth said. "And you promised not to tell Mom. You lied to me."

"We saved your butt. You're welcome."

He shut the first aid kit. "Whatever. Sew yourself up. Stitch your eyes closed and bleed to death if you want. I don't care."

"I'm not joking. Rylie will kill you," Abel said.

"At least she doesn't lie to me."

Abel craned his neck to the side to examine his injury. When he couldn't see it, he jumped off the counter and moved for the bathroom. He staggered drunkenly and barely caught himself on the empty refrigerator.

"Whoa!"

"Sit down, stupid. You're going to kill yourself before Rylie can finish the job," Seth said.

Abel did sit down—on the floor. Hard. He tried to grab the table on his way down and managed to pull the first aid kit on his head. Seth grabbed the needle and scissors off the floor before he could hurt himself.

"This cheap trailer is such a piece of crap! The floor isn't even level!" Abel snarled.

Seth didn't argue even though the floor was fine. He rinsed out a cup of soda from a burger joint, filling it with water from the tap, and handed it to his brother. "Drink it."

"Sure, *Mom.*"

Eleanor had never been the type to watch over them when they were sick, and they both knew it. The joke fell flat.

Abel chugged the entire thing in one breath, wiping water off his chin. Seth knelt beside him to examine the bite wound. "I'm going to have to put a bandage on it. I don't think we can stitch the rest. You're going to have a really bad scar."

"Your girlfriend has a hell of a bite on her."

"I told you, she's not my girlfriend!"

"Good." Abel gripped Seth's shoulders in both hands. "Listen to me, bro. I protected you tonight. You're an idiot, but we're family, so we'll have this mushy talk once. All right?" No response. "Werewolves killed Dad. A werewolf almost turned me. I don't want to see you bitten or dead."

Seth smacked a gauze pad on the wound and taped it down, then shoved his brother toward bed. "You should sleep."

For once, he didn't argue. Abel collapsed on top of a pile of sheets in the corner. They didn't have mattresses. Buying beds didn't kill werewolves.

Seth was so used to his mom's Spartan approach to life that he usually didn't think twice about it, but watching his injured brother trying to find a comfortable position on the floor made a knot of anger clench in his stomach.

"Think I'm going to turn into a werewolf on the next moon?" Abel mumbled into the sweater he used as a pillow.

It was a question Seth had been trying not to consider. He didn't think anybody had been bitten by a werewolf twice before. So he didn't respond.

"Rylie is different," he said as he shut the door. "She is."

Abel snored.

Seth stood on the porch, craning his neck back to search the sky for a moon. Moths fluttered through the air, and the light on the porch occasionally crackled and snapped as one drew too close and fried on the electrified wire. It was late enough at night to be considered early morning.

Rylie was out there, and so was his mom.

He didn't want to think about what they were doing.

If Seth was supposed to be an amazing hunter like Dad—destined to save humanity from the werewolf threat—then why was his life so miserable? Why did he have to grow up in a family where it was normal to live in an apartment without heat or electricity? What kind of people survived off nothing but a dwindling life insurance policy?

Why should Seth have to grow up in motels with a mom bent on hunting when Rylie had designer clothes and a family who loved her?

He didn't deserve it. Any of it.

It was all too horrible for him to take. Misery overwhelmed and choked him. He sank to the steps and pressed his forehead to his knees.

Seth didn't move until the sun rose.

•◯•

By the time dawn stretched over the horizon, Eleanor hadn't gotten to kill anything.

She hadn't so much as glimpsed the werewolf since it jumped the fence. She found signs of it, yes—broken trees, paw prints twice the breadth of human feet, and even a rabbit with a snapped neck. But no matter how fast she moved, she couldn't catch up with the beast.

The only mercy was that her chase had led them away from civilization. The blood smears she found were stuck with rabbit fur, not human hair.

"Still not a good sign, is it, honey?" she asked the clouds. She imagined Jim, her dead husband, watching the hunt from Heaven. She was never sure if it was a happy thought. He had been a hard man to satisfy. None of her kills were as good as his, and he was always happy to tell her that she could never replicate his techniques with any skill.

She wondered what he would think of the werewolf escaping her. Eleanor was sure he would have gotten it already.

Her search led her in a loop around the hills and back to the mine. It was unlikely that the wolf would have gone back to the place it turned once its den had been compromised, so she shouldered her rifle before hopping the fence.

Eleanor shone a flashlight around the cement as she went down the stairs in the mine. She didn't care about the heavy machinery left behind by the corporation that owned it, even though the parts might have been valuable. She focused on the ground. A werewolf's claws weren't sharp enough to score concrete when it walked, but there was always blood where they transformed.

When she found the first smears of crimson, she tracked them back to an empty room with a heavy door that had been ripped from its hinges.

A lantern was tipped on its side in the corner. Eleanor righted it, frowning at the broken bulb and the scuffed casing. She had a similar lantern at home, but that didn't seem too odd. Anybody could buy them at a corner store.

A glimmer of something lighter than the rest of the floor caught her eye, and she knelt to get a closer look.

Hair. Human hair.

They were like long, silvery strands of moonlight, and they made Eleanor's heart race as she turned them over in her fingers.

Long hair probably meant a woman. A blond woman.

"Now what do you think of that, Jim?" she asked. He probably would have laughed and gone to sharpen his knives. He liked to skin the werewolves and keep the pelts as a trophy.

Looping the hairs around her hand, she tucked them into a pouch on her belt and stood. Her search had just become much easier.

Eleanor left the mine grinning.

She had been awake for almost thirty-six hours and fatigue weighed heavy on her bones, but she wasn't ready to sleep. How many women with pale blond hair could possibly live in such a small town?

Her sons must have taken the car back to the trailer. The only sign it had been parked there were tire tracks. She found Abel's motorcycle hidden in the bushes and mounted it, leaving the helmet hanging from a saddlebag.

Eleanor thought about blond hair as she roared down the road.

Was it blond in color, or gray? It was hard to tell the difference. If it was gray, then Gwyneth Gresham would be the main suspect.

Only one way to find out.

She went straight to the Gresham ranch and was surprised to find the Chevy parked on the hill. Eleanor tried to remember how badly Abel had been injured the night before. The werewolf had definitely bitten him, so it seemed doubtful he would have gone to work.

Parking the motorcycle behind a tree where it wouldn't be visible from the house, Eleanor climbed into the branches to wait for Gwyneth to emerge. She didn't have to wait long. The woman came out wearing leather gloves with her graying blond hair pulled into two thick braids. She had a shovel in one hand.

She didn't look like a woman who had spent her night mauling rabbits.

Eleanor pulled out the hair to give it another look in the sunlight. It was shinier and more silken than Gwyneth Gresham's hair. Definitely blond, not silver.

Then why was her son's car parked there?

Gwyneth went into the barn, and noise drew Eleanor's attention to the other side of the hill. To her surprise, she saw Seth pacing by the pond.

I'm hunting. Isn't that what he said the night before? Maybe he had found the hair, too.

She had been surprised when Seth wanted to spend the summer hunting werewolves alone—proud, but surprised. Yet he seemed more reluctant to embrace his destiny when he returned. He'd become even more stubborn and talked a lot about college.

He wasn't the boy she thought she raised. He was nothing like his father.

"Didn't we always fear the teenage rebellion?" she whispered to Jim. Abel was a good kid. He was almost as dedicated as Eleanor. But Seth... he was a disappointment.

He suddenly straightened and rushed down the hill. Eleanor narrowed her eyes to see what he was running toward.

A pale figure limped out of the fields.

Eleanor dropped out of the tree and crouch-walked into the garden to get a closer look.

It was a girl. She was probably Seth's age, and naked as the day God brought her onto the Earth. Her skin was filthy. One of her legs was pouring blood.

And her hair was a shimmering white-gold sheet down her back.

"Seth," she said, her voice thick with tears. Her chest hitched. "I think I got shot."

She dropped, and he caught her. "Oh my God."

Oh my God.

A sense of calm settled over Eleanor as she took in the scene in front of her. The girl—blond-haired and naked the morning after a new moon—must have been the monster. That part didn't require much thinking. Eleanor heard Gwyneth had a niece living on her ranch. Abel had spoken the name "Rylie" once or twice himself.

But the way his son held that beast, looking at her with tenderness as he felt her leg… now *that* was something wrong.

If she thought she had been disappointed in Seth before, it was nothing in comparison to the way she felt now.

"You're healing," he said. "I think the bullet passed through. You should be okay."

"It burns," she whimpered.

"It's the silver in the bullets. That's why it's closing so slowly. If we clean out the wound—"

"Where's Gwyn? Help me get inside. She can't see."

Eleanor didn't want to hear any more of it. She stroked a hand down the butt of her rifle. Jim's voice came echoing from the dim depths of her memory. *We don't kill them when they're humans.*

But oh, it was tempting. So very tempting.

Now she knew. And it wouldn't be long until the next moon.

Thirteen

A Visitor

Rylie's thigh was on fire. She could barely move her leg. She dressed slowly in the bathroom while Seth hid in her bedroom, pulling a flowered sundress over her head. Jeans would have hurt too much.

Scrubbing her hands and arms in the sink, she got as much dirt off her upper body as she could manage before grabbing a spare towel and limping back to her room. Seth stood up when she came through the door.

"What happened? Did my mom find you?"

"I don't know," Rylie said. She laid the towel on her bed and sat on it, pressing a hand to her forehead as she tried to remember. The night before was as foggy as the rest of her nights as a werewolf. She groaned. "I don't know! Why can't I remember being a werewolf?"

He knelt in front of her. "It's normal. There's nothing wrong with you. Can I see your leg?"

Rylie bit her lip and nodded, lifting the hem of her skirt. The injury was kind of high on her thigh. Her blush almost burned more than the silver alloy did.

Seth leaned in close enough that she could feel his breath warming her skin. Her heart hammered.

Her excitement disappeared the instant his fingers probed the wound. Rylie squeezed her eyes shut as pain throbbed through her. It felt like getting stabbed in the hip.

"Silver is a soft metal," Seth said as he examined her, sounding totally calm again. "The bullets are cast with other metals to inflict maximum damage. They're supposed to sit in the injury and leech silver in your veins until you die of poisoning."

"I thought you said the bullet passed through!"

He gestured for her to lean to the side, and he looked at the other side of her leg. "It did. You were lucky."

Lucky. Funny choice of words. Rylie hugged a pillow to her chest, digging her fingernails into the stuffing. "How do we clean it?" she asked. She had broken bones since getting bitten over the summer, and they healed within minutes after a flush of heat. This burning kept getting worse instead of better.

"The back has closed. The front hasn't." Seth gripped her hand in his. "We can wait for the silver to pass through on its own. There isn't much, or else you wouldn't be walking at all."

"How long?"

"Days. Maybe weeks."

She groaned. "I have to go to school, Seth! And Gwyn can't find out I got shot. She'll go nuts!"

"I can pull the fragments out now," he said.

Her eyes burned with tears. "I don't know if I can do that."

"I'll be fast. Do you have tweezers?"

Rylie pointed to the vanity. Seth searched through her drawers until he came up with a pair of needle-point tweezers, which she had used to pluck her eyebrows until she realized her hair was too pale for anyone to tell if she had one eyebrow or two.

"Will it hurt?" she whispered.

"Yeah." Seth pulled a lighter out of his pocket and flicked the igniter, holding the end of the tweezers in the flame. "Why don't you stretch out?"

She felt like she was going to hyperventilate. She made herself focus on the white ceiling so she wouldn't see what he was doing with the tweezers.

"Do you do this a lot?"

"You mean, fix people up?" he asked. "Yeah. Just last night, Abel and I…" He trailed off, hand resting on her leg. She could hear a roaring in her ears like the icy waterfalls on Gray Mountain.

"Last night? What happened last night?"

"You bit Abel."

"*What?*"

Fire exploded all up and down her leg. Rylie mashed the pillow onto her face to smother the sounds of pain. It only lasted a moment, but when Seth withdrew the tweezers, it was burning even worse than before. Her whole body shook with sobs.

"You have to hold still, Rylie. There's still something in there."

"No, don't—"

He inserted the tweezers into her injury again.

This time, she couldn't smother her scream.

She flushed hot when he withdrew them. A wildfire of pain rolled up and down her body. Her thigh muscle shook. It was nothing like the other times she had super-healed a broken bone or scrape. Rylie felt nothing but pain. It blinded her to the world.

Seth climbed into bed and pulled her into his arms.

She wasn't sure how long it took the pain to stop. It could have been a few seconds, or it could have been hours. But eventually, it did stop. Her leg gave another spasm and grew still.

Rylie sagged against him. She knew she must have looked totally gross, but she couldn't make herself care.

"I don't want to do this anymore," she whispered.

"Hey," he murmured against the top of her head. "I'll help you. We'll figure it out together."

"I don't want to die."

"You're not going to die. I promise."

They sat together in silence for a few minutes as her pulse slowed and her breathing became normal again. He used the edge of the towel to wipe the blood off Rylie's leg, and she saw that the injury had closed completely.

Seth helped her sit up. Rylie tugged her skirt down. Now that she wasn't in pain, she was kind of embarrassed to have a boy in her room. It should have been a little exciting, too, but pulling a bullet out of her leg wasn't exactly thrilling.

"Is Abel okay?" she asked.

"He's alive."

"What does biting him again mean? Will he be a werewolf now?"

"I don't know. I don't think anybody has ever resisted the change before, and then got bitten again." He cleaned the blood off his hands with the towel. "He's tough. He'll be fine."

"I'm so sorry," she said.

"You don't have to pretend to care. I know you hate him."

"But I didn't want to hurt him. If he starts to change again, I want to do something about it. I want to help him."

"I don't know if you can." Seth stood up. "I should go see him. If he's healed already, then it probably means he'll change. If the bite is still open, then he should be safe."

"What are we going to do about your family? They saw me. They know I'm here. I don't know how we can make them leave me alone now."

"I don't know." Seth ran a hand over his hair. "I just… I don't know."

He left, and she waited until he snuck out the back door to try to stand up again. Even though her leg felt better, she was still weak. Seth had left the tweezers and a couple pebble-sized bits of silver on the floor. It was hard to believe something so small could have caused so much pain.

Wobbling out to the kitchen, Rylie found leftovers from the last couple of dinners. The fridge was packed full of steaks and roasts and ribs. She knew Gwyn would probably make breakfast later, but she couldn't wait to eat. Her body demanded food.

Rylie pulled an entire rack of ribs out of the refrigerator and heated it up in the microwave while she tore into a cold steak. Her body revolted at the taste of it. She wanted something warm and fresh, and the image of a rabbit flashed through her mind. She ignored it.

Someone knocked at the door. Rylie paused mid-bite, slowly chewing what she had in her mouth.

Who would visit so early on the weekend? Nobody who came to the house knocked. The ranch hands—even Abel—knew they were welcome to walk in and out as freely as family.

The knocking repeated, and Rylie set her steak on the counter to limp into the living room. Maybe Gwyn locked herself out.

She found a statuesque woman standing on the other side of the door. She had the same strong nose and dark eyes as Seth, so Rylie immediately recognized her as his mom. What had he called her? Eleanor?

"What do you…?" Rylie started to ask.

Eleanor lashed out and grabbed a fistful of Rylie's hair in her fist, yanking her onto the step.

Shrieking, Rylie clawed at the hand with her fingernails, but she lost balance and fell to her knees. Eleanor dragged her through the dirt screaming.

"Gwyn! Help me!"

"Shut your mouth," Eleanor said, tossing Rylie against the motorcycle and backhanding her. Her head snapped to the side. The taste of iron flooded her mouth.

The wolf was always quiet after a moon, and the silver only made it worse. It was exhausted. Rylie had no strength.

She tried to dodge Eleanor's next blow, but it connected with her jaw as she tried to get to her feet. She fell to the ground again. Rylie opened her mouth to yell and the older woman clapped her hand over her mouth.

It was then that her eyes fell on the black ropes at Eleanor's belt. Panic swelled inside of her.

The adrenaline stirred the wolf, giving her a small burst of strength. Rylie ripped out of her grip and shoved her hard enough to send her flying.

Leaping to her feet, she bolted down the hill.

Her first instinct was to run to Gwyneth, who had a shotgun, but she knew just as quickly that she couldn't do it. Her aunt had no problem shooting coyotes, but she would hesitate to shoot a person. Eleanor wouldn't think twice before pulling her own trigger.

She couldn't let Gwyn get killed.

Eleanor was getting to her feet. Those ropes looked like death waiting to happen.

Rylie's bare feet slapped against the dirt as the motorcycle growled to life behind her. It blasted in a circle and blocked her route down the road, kicking gravel into her face.

She tried to run the other way, but Eleanor zoomed past her, and she snatched at Rylie's hair again. She threw herself to the ground and felt a fistful of hair rip from her scalp. Rylie cried out and scrambled to her knees.

If she could just get into the bushes by the side of the road—

The motorcycle roared toward her. She rolled onto her side and felt the tire blow past her head.

When she sat up, she saw Eleanor wheeling around for another pass. Scrambling to her feet, Rylie leaped over the split rail fence and bolted across the pasture as fast as she could. Her leg throbbed with silver poisoning.

The motorcycle raced down the path between fields.

Cutting across the fields, Rylie took the shortest route she knew toward town. Terror blinded her. The world blurred. She had never moved so fast in her life.

All Rylie could think was *I need Seth* over and over. She didn't know what else to do.

Something struck her in the back and bowled her over. She hit the dirt face first. All of her breath rushed out of her lungs, and she gasped, gripping her chest.

Eleanor stopped the motorcycle and jumped down. Rylie tried to crawl away, but the older woman pinned her down and wrapped the ropes around her wrists. "Stop!" Rylie wheezed. "Wait—what are—"

"Don't talk to me."

She twisted the black ropes all the way up Rylie's arms. Eleanor knotted them and dragged her to the motorcycle. The weeds tore at Rylie's dress.

Twisting around, she tried to kick herself free.

"Let me go!" she cried. Eleanor sat on the motorcycle again and wrapped the other end of the rope around the handle. Her foot kicked off the brake. "No!"

Her arms nearly ripped out of her sockets when the bike leaped forward. Her shoulders screamed. Fire burned on the side of her body as dirt scraped up her side. Eleanor didn't drive fast—she didn't mean to kill Rylie. But it burned even worse than the silver.

Rylie thrashed, but the ropes were too tight. She couldn't get free.

The world shot past her at ten miles an hour.

Her body bumped over a rock. A cut split open on her shoulder.

The dirt scraped her skin raw even as the healing fever swept over her. She was injured and healed over and over again while Eleanor drove toward town, cutting through gaps in the fence to skip from pasture to pasture.

Rylie screamed until her throat felt like it was hamburger meat. Eleanor glanced at her.

"I told you to shut up," she snapped, turning the handle of the motorcycle.

Her head smashed into a rock.

Rylie's screams cut off. Everything went gray and fuzzy.

She wasn't sure how long Eleanor dragged her behind the motorcycle. Her aunt owned a lot of land between their house and town. It felt like they went on for miles, but she knew that Eleanor had to reach the perimeter of the ranch soon. She *had* to.

The motorcycle finally stopped, and Rylie lay facedown on the ground shivering. The grains of dirt looked like boulders in her hazy vision.

Eleanor's footsteps moved toward the fence. She heard the creaking of the gate.

It was her only chance.

Pushing herself forward to make the rope slack, Rylie ripped her arms apart and buried her fingernails into the rope. It frayed and snapped.

"Hey!" Eleanor shouted.

Rylie was free of the motorcycle, but she couldn't get her arms apart. She swung her fists together and struck Eleanor in the face, sending her the ground.

She didn't wait to see if she had hit hard enough.

Vaulting over the fence, Rylie stumbled onto a farm and stripped the ropes from her arms. They weren't far from town.

She dodged into the cornfields, ears perked for the sound of a motorcycle engine, and stuck to the back of the fields so the farmer wouldn't see her. A lot of corn had already been picked. It didn't leave her much coverage.

Bursting through a wall of corn, Rylie leaped back in time to avoid a yellow harvester.

She could see the road. She was almost there.

And Eleanor's motorcycle came roaring around the corner.

Rylie darted across the street. A hand stretched through the air, reaching for her back, but she ducked just in time to miss the swipe.

She climbed a chain link fence and dropped to the other side. Eleanor buzzed past.

Since she had never come into town from the wrong side of the strip mall before, Rylie was disoriented. Where was Seth's trailer park? She didn't have time to figure it out. Eleanor was coming around to the other side.

A group of women in blue jeans dropped their shopping bags when Rylie flew past them. There was a restaurant across the parking lot, and someone she knew was standing in front of it. He was wearing his normal polo shirt and smoking something that didn't look quite like a cigarette.

"Tate!" Rylie cried. "Help me!"

He blinked at her. "What?"

Tate focused over her shoulder and saw the motorcycle roaring through the parking lot. It was like a splash of cold water. He grabbed her and dove into the alley between the restaurant and the shopping center.

"Run!" she shrieked.

But there was nowhere to go at the end. Eleanor maneuvered the motorcycle in front of the alley and leaped off.

The only way out was a dark door tagged with graffiti. Tate threw it open and they dove inside, slamming it shut behind them. Eleanor's fists pounded on the door and the knob rattled, and then it went silent.

They were in a dark restaurant storeroom. Rylie's back was pressed against a box of napkins. She realized Tate was staring at her, his eyes reflecting the light from the kitchen, and she glanced down. Her entire body was covered in blood and mud.

"I'll explain later," Rylie wheezed. "She's going to go around front."

"There's another door out back. That way!"

They ran through the kitchen. A portly woman in an apron gave them a brief look before going back to tossing her pizza dough. Rylie had to wonder what kind of things Tate did that meant nobody bat an eye at him running through their restaurant like he was being chased by a tiger.

At that moment, she didn't really care. They burst out of the security gate to find Tate's old BMW backed up to the restaurant. Rylie threw herself in the passenger's seat as he started the engine. It reeked so strongly of marijuana that she felt like she had jumped into a bong.

"Where should I go?" he asked.

Eleanor rounded the side of the building.

"I don't care! Just go! Go!"

He gunned it. They peeled out of the parking lot. Rylie twisted around to watch the street receding behind them.

"That was nuts," Tate said, giggling madly. "Cool. So cool. I knew you were going to be awesome when I saw you." He tore down the streets, weaving crazily between the lanes and hopping on the curb every time he turned a corner.

There was no motorcycle behind them. They had lost her.

"She wants to kill me," Rylie said.

"No way."

"Seriously."

Tate started laughing harder. She would have been annoyed if the shock of it didn't suddenly sink in. Every inch of Rylie shook, and she bowed her head against her knees as she dug her fingernails into her shoulders.

Eleanor tried to kill her.

Twice.

Her body had already healed from getting dragged through the fields, but the memory of it haunted her. She kept seeing the grass dragging past her head and feeling the rash of the dirt scraping a long line down her body.

She gave a hiccupping sob. Before Rylie became a werewolf, she hadn't even broken a bone before. Now she was getting shot and beaten and she had no idea how to handle it.

Tate noticed Rylie starting to cry, and he got the wild look of a cornered animal. "Whoa, don't do that. You mean it? She's really trying to kill you?"

"You think I would joke about that?" Rylie snapped.

"Who was that bitch? She looked like a freaking Terminator."

"I don't want to talk about it."

"All right, all right, don't freak out. There's no panic in the Tate Zone. We're cool here. Deep breaths."

Being told to take deep breaths only made her angrier, but the shock overwhelmed everything else. "Fine," Rylie ground out between her teeth. "We're cool."

"Is your face okay?"

"My face?"

She pulled down the visor to look in the mirror. Blood caked the entire right side of her face from hairline to jaw. It looked like she should have been skinned, but it was smooth and uninjured underneath.

Rylie couldn't feel surprised or horrified. She couldn't feel anything at all.

Her hands shook as she pushed the visor up again.

"I hit my head when I was running."

"You need a doctor?" he asked.

"No."

"Cool. You can hide out at my folks' place," he said. "The whole basement is the Tate Zone. They never go down there, and you can chill as long as you want."

"You don't think I should call the cops or something?"

"No! No. Don't do that. Those pigs aren't good for anything," he said.

He probably had a point. Rylie didn't think they were out to get her—although they might have been out to get Tate, considering his hobbies—but she didn't think they could help her with a supernatural problem. Would they even believe her if she said she was a werewolf with a hunter chasing her down?

The worst part was that Rylie wasn't sure who they would side with if they did believe her.

As adrenaline faded, exhaustion took its place. She seldom slept on her nights as a werewolf. Rylie almost passed out in Tate's BMW before they reached his house.

Like most people, he lived a few miles out of town, but his community was in a gated development on an artificial lake. He keyed in the code and drove up to a huge house with a circular driveway, well-manicured lawn, and topiaries.

"Is this where you live?" Rylie asked. She hadn't known there were any rich people in her farming community.

"Yeah. Boring, huh?"

He pulled into a garage beneath the house, and Rylie got out on trembling legs. The "Tate Zone" turned out to be more like a roomy apartment beneath his parent's house than a basement, which looked into their immaculate yard with huge windows.

"What do you parents do?"

"They own half the crappy farms around here. My mom's the county commissioner." Tate sounded like he cared about it as much as he would have cared about a sobriety program.

His living space was covered in piles of clothes and marijuana paraphernalia, some of which was arranged on his walls like glass-blown works of art. Cans of empty Red Bull were scattered everywhere, and everything felt like it was covered in a thin layer of grime.

Beneath his mess, though, were platinum fixtures, and he had a chandelier and a baby grand piano that he looked to be using as a laundry hanger.

"This is all yours?" she asked, running a hand over an antique table with a giant sticker of Bob Marley pasted to the surface.

"Yup." He opened a box on his bookshelf, which was full of classic literature that looked well-read. He took a joint and lighter out of the box and shut it again. "My parents are on some trip to Singapore, so you can do whatever."

"Thanks," Rylie said. "Really. Thank you."

"Yup." He plopped in a chair in front of a flat screen TV wider than Rylie was tall. "Want to watch a movie and smoke?"

"Actually... is there somewhere I can sleep?"

"Sure. Guest room." He waved in the direction of the piano.

The room was cleaner than the rest of his living space, other than a couple of guitars propped against the wall. It looked like he never went inside. The bed was clean and curtains kept it dark, so it was all Rylie needed.

She dropped on the bed and immediately fell asleep.

Fourteen

The Tate Zone

When Rylie woke up, it was dark outside, and she felt stiff and dirty. She got out of bed to find Tate unconscious in front of his TV, which was looping a menu on his Star Wars Blu-ray.

She was starving, although the clock showed her it wasn't as late as it felt. It was barely dinnertime. Aunt Gwyneth was probably starting to wonder what had happened to her, but she wasn't sure if it would be safe to call.

Rylie didn't want to call her aunt, who wouldn't be able to do anything about the hunter on her trail. She wanted to call Seth. She was pretty sure he didn't have a phone, though.

Searching for a bathroom, Rylie found one near the stairs with a tub the size of a small swimming pool. It was totally gross. The sink was full of hair, and it looked like Tate didn't have very good aim around the toilet.

She fidgeted uncomfortably in the doorway for a good three minutes before deciding that her need to use the bathroom wasn't as bad as her need not to sit on that disgusting toilet seat.

Tate snorted in his recliner when she came out.

"Hey," she whispered, touching his shoulder.

He jerked awake. "Who? What?"

"It's me. Sorry. I need to know…"

"What are you doing here?" He wrinkled his nose. "We didn't have sex, did we?"

"What? God, no!" Rylie pulled up on the neck of her tattered dress self-consciously. She tried not to look repulsed by the thought so she wouldn't hurt his feelings, but unfortunately, Tate looked relieved at her answer.

"Oh. Cool. What's up?"

"Do you have another bathroom?"

"Yeah. And don't take this the wrong way, but you could seriously use a shower. You look horrible," he said.

It was hard to be offended when she knew he was right. She looked like she had been dragged for ten miles behind a motorcycle—which she had.

Tate led her upstairs. It was gorgeous. Rylie's family did pretty well, but his parents must have been millionaires to afford a house with so much marble. They had the kind of art that needed to be kept behind glass. It looked like they had a maid, too, because there was no hint of Tate's squalor from the basement.

He took her to a bathroom that was like his, but much cleaner. "Thanks," she said.

"I think my mom's about your size. Want something clean to wear?" he asked. When Rylie hesitated, he said, "She has a closet bigger than my basement. She won't notice."

"Sure."

He ducked into his parent's room and came back with a blue dress that looked like it had been tailored specifically for his mom. It was really pretty, but cut for an older woman with a high neckline and three-quarter sleeves. Rylie fingered the beadwork around the waist and wondered how much it cost. She liked to wear designers, but having people make clothes for her would have been something else entirely.

"I'll be downstairs," Tate said, disappearing.

She scrubbed herself clean in the shower, using every type of body wash. The dirt and blood swirled around the drain in red-black clouds. She had to shampoo her hair three times to get all the sticky stuff out, and by the time she was done, her entire body glistened red from having been rubbed too hard.

Rylie tried not to remember being dragged behind the motorcycle. It made her want to start crying again, and she was done crying.

What was wrong with Eleanor? Who would do something like that?

Her chin trembled with the beginning of tears, but she closed her eyes and took deep breaths until it stopped.

The towels on the shelf were so fluffy that Rylie could have slept in them. By the time she combed out her hair with her fingers and pulled the dress over her head, she almost felt human again.

Tate's mom was shorter than Rylie, and her chest was bigger too. The skirt was a little too short and it was baggy at the top. It was still a pretty dress. There wasn't even a mark on her leg where she had gotten shot earlier.

She plucked at the beads as she studied herself in the mirror. Seth had told her the only way to escape his family would be to run. But where was she supposed to go? Going to live with her aunt had been how she ran away from her old life. She didn't have any other ideas.

Tate was moving around the kitchen when she got out. It looked like he had showered, too. He was wearing a clean polo and khakis, and his eyes weren't as red as usual.

"You hungry?" he asked, grabbing a loaf of bread and sandwich meat out of the fridge.

Her stomach gave a sharp cramp at the mention. "Starving. But could I borrow your phone first?"

"No problem." Tate took a phone off the wall and tossed it to her. "How high was I this morning?"

"Pretty high."

He laughed. "I must have been a ten. I think that new stuff was laced with something. My head weighs, like, a million pounds." He dropped the food on the counter and went back for more. "Are you John Connor? Why did she want you dead?"

"It's probably better if we don't talk about it."

"Cool. Whatever."

Rylie took the phone out to the garden to call. Gwyn picked up on the first ring.

"Rylie?"

"It's me," she said. "I'm okay." Gwyn sighed with relief, and Rylie immediately felt guilty. "I'm sorry I disappeared."

"Where have you been?"

"It's a long story. I'm with one of my friends now."

"A boyfriend?"

"No. Um, something kind of bad has happened, and I don't want you to panic or anything, but I don't think I should come home right now."

Her aunt's voice sharpened. "What is it?"

"It's really hard to explain."

"Did you get into trouble with that stoner friend?"

"No, it's… I don't know. You wouldn't believe me," Rylie said. "I want to tell you. I do. But I can't come home. I'm going to hang out here for the weekend, and I'll…" She swallowed. "I'll give you a call later."

"Tell me where you are right now. Don't hang up."

"I'm sorry, Gwyn," she said.

She stared at the phone in her hand long after she disconnected. The truth was, she hadn't given a lot of thought to what she would do after the call. Rylie couldn't stay with Tate forever. His parents would come home eventually, and it wouldn't be a safe place to transform on the next moon anyway.

Inside, Tate had set up a sandwich factory on the counter, and he was in the middle of constructing his third sandwich.

There were crumbs everywhere. He handed Rylie a plate without asking any questions, for which she was grateful. She had been on the verge of tears since she woke up, and she was afraid that talking would get her sobbing.

Rylie got a heaping serving of meat, and they sat at a dining room table that looked like it was meant for fancy dinner parties to eat.

It was the first time she had ever seen Tate sober. He actually looked like a normal guy.

"I hate this room," he said. "I've had to go to a hundred stupid fundraisers here. Politics is my mom's whole life. I think she wants to be president someday."

"Sorry," Rylie said.

"They think I'm embarrassing. They don't invite me to their parties anymore. I'm supposed to shut up and stay downstairs." He laughed. "It's probably better like that."

"I don't think I'd enjoy dinner parties with politicians anyway."

"No kidding." Tate put the rest of his second sandwich in his mouth and swallowed it down. He practically inhaled his food. It was the one thing that all of her guy friends had in common— they all ate like starving hyenas. "You're really weird."

Rylie paused in the middle of shredding some turkey. "Uh… thanks?"

"I just downloaded some new games. Want to play?"

The idea of doing something so casual in the middle of hiding away from a murderous hunter was so ridiculous she had to laugh. "Yeah. Sure."

They took their food downstairs. Rylie had never played a video game in her entire life, so she died about a hundred times in the first hour. They connected with Tate's other friends online, and all three of them proceeded to tease and insult her for hours. The controls were awkward. Rylie's hands felt more like paws, so she was too clumsy to maneuver properly.

She had to admit she was really awful and gave up around the time the sun rose, but Rylie hung out on one of Tate's leather couches with a headset to watch and laugh with them.

It was dumb, but it was so relaxing. It let her forget about silver bullets and black motorcycles for a couple of hours.

By the time they signed off, Rylie was perfectly comfortable in the Tate Zone. She half-wished she could hide in his basement forever.

But dawn reminded her of Gwyn, and all the work that needed to be done around the ranch.

Tate noticed that she was getting antsy. "Maybe you should call your aunt again," he suggested. "You can stay here and all, but I bet she misses you."

"Yeah. I guess."

"Want me to take you home?"

Rylie nodded reluctantly. She didn't want to go back—she imagined Eleanor waiting for her there with those black ropes. But if she was going to have to leave, she needed to pack some of her clothes. She couldn't run off with all of the county commissioner's wardrobe.

Tate was yawning as he drove her out to the ranch. Gwyn met them at the bottom of the hill.

"Thanks for everything," Rylie told him before opening the door. "You can go. You don't want to face my aunt's wrath."

"All right."

He was practically gone before she could shut the door.

Gwyn took off her hat and studied Rylie's unfamiliar dress with a twisted mouth. "I found a bloody towel in your room and half-cooked food in the kitchen. Looked like you left in a hurry. Want to tell me what that's about?"

"No," Rylie said.

"Let's get inside where it's warm," Gwyn said. She didn't look angry. She looked as tired as Rylie felt.

"No. I can't stay for long. I have to leave."

Her aunt dusted her hat off on her knee. "And where do you think you're going?" she asked, concentrating very hard on a smudge of dirt near the brim.

"I don't know, but it's not safe here."

"Why?"

"That's the problem. I can't tell you."

Gwyn put the hat on again, studying her niece with a grave expression. "It seems we have a trust problem, babe. I know something is happening with you, but you won't tell me what. I know you've never gotten along with your mom, but I thought it'd be different with me. Guess you've never had an adult you could trust."

"I did once," Rylie admitted. "Her name was Louise, and she was a counselor at Camp Silver Brook. She wanted to help me."

"This is about camp?"

"Yeah… and no. Everything in my life is kind of about camp now."

"Is Louise one of the counselors who got killed?"

She nodded. "She kept giving me chances, and I kept screwing them up. I let her down. I wish I could fix it, but I didn't even get to apologize to her before she…" Rylie swallowed. "Camp was awful. This whole summer was awful."

"I know," Gwyn said. "Those bear attacks did a lot of harm."

"There weren't any bears. Not a single one."

"That's what the news said."

"The news lied," Rylie said. Her aunt watched her, waiting for her to go on. "It was… something else. Something even worse."

The wind blew around them. Gwyn folded her arms. Rylie couldn't tell if she believed her or not, because her expression had gone stony.

"What was it?" she asked.

"It was a werewolf."

All Hallows' Moon

The silence got much, much heavier.

"A... werewolf," Gwyn said.

Rylie went on in a rush. "It bit me, so I'm a werewolf now too." She couldn't stand to see the disbelief on her aunt's face. "I've been turning into a wolf every new and full moon for weeks. There's these people, these hunters. They're out to get me. One of them came to kill me and I had to run. That's why I have to leave."

"Rylie..."

"I'm serious, Gwyn. I'm not making it up."

Her aunt rubbed her face. "I know you're not trying to lie to me. This is... well, not what I expected. I thought you were going to tell me you got into drugs or pregnant or something. That's something I could handle. But... werewolves?"

She looked down at her hands. "Yeah."

"And... do you have any proof?"

"Sure. On the next full moon."

Gwyn fanned herself with her hat. She was taking a lot of deep breaths. "Jesus, Rylie. Are you trying to tell me you killed those people at camp?"

"No! That was the guy who bit me. It was this counselor named Jericho. I was out wandering one night, and he attacked me, and after that..." It sounded so stupid that she couldn't finish the sentence. "He killed everyone."

"And now you want to run away."

"I don't *want* to," she said. "But the hunters will get me if I don't."

"Okay," Gwyn said. She took out her keys. "Let's get in the truck and get going."

"Okay? You believe me?"

"Sure," she said very, very gently. "I believe you."

"We have to hurry."

"I know."

They got into the truck. Rylie couldn't believe it. There was no way Gwyn could accept that she had become a werewolf so easily. She had been bitten months ago and she still didn't believe it sometimes. But she didn't care as long as they got on the move and stayed away from Eleanor. She could help convince Gwyn later.

"Where are we going to go?" Rylie asked as they left the ranch.

"Somewhere safe. It sounds like there's a lot you need to talk about, babe."

They didn't go toward town. They turned the other way instead. Rylie felt better as they got further away from the ranch, and being with Gwyn again helped too. There wasn't much more comforting than having her tough aunt and a shotgun on a rack in the truck.

Staying up with Tate all night left her drowsy, so Rylie dozed in the front seat as they drove for an hour.

The farms and countryside began to turn into suburbs. It was after noon when they reached another town. It was bigger than the one where Rylie attended school. There was a real mall, a ten-screen movie theater, and a lot of restaurants.

"I'm hungry," Rylie said.

"We'll get lunch soon."

Gwyneth pulled up to a white building with a big sign in the front. It said "St. Philomene's Regional Hospital" in tall letters. She was so confused when her aunt stopped in the parking lot that she didn't move at first.

"What are we doing at a hospital?" she asked.

Her aunt took her hand. "Listen to yourself, Rylie. You're talking werewolves and assault and conspiracies. I think... I think what hit you this summer hit you hard. You're having a tough time with reality. Jessica should have put you straight into counseling."

The meaning of what she said struck Rylie. "You think I'm crazy?"

"No," Gwyn said forcefully. "No. You're not. But you said it yourself. You saw something awful this summer, and I think it confused you. You need to talk to some kind of professional and get yourself sorted."

"So you're going to put me in the psychiatric ward?" Rylie's voice rose in pitch until she was almost shrieking. "I'm not crazy, Gwyn! I can't get locked up! What if I—I mean—" A tear rolled down her cheek, and she swiped it away with a hand. "I trusted you!"

Rylie threw open the door, but Gwyn's voice stopped her. "Where are going to go?"

"I don't know. Somewhere else! You can't lock me up!"

Her aunt hopped out of the truck and followed her as she ran across the parking lot. Rylie stopped when she reached the street. Tears rolled freely down her cheeks.

"Babe," Gwyn said gently. "Think about it. If what you said is true, you can't go home anyway. There's people to watch you in the hospital. Nobody can hurt you there. I'll stay with you, okay? I won't leave you alone."

"This is stupid. I won't do it."

"Just talk to someone. Please."

Her aunt was right. She couldn't go back to the ranch, and unless Rylie wanted to stay with Tate forever, she had nowhere to go.

But the thought of institutionalization terrified her. What if they kept her longer than two weeks and she became a werewolf in the psychiatric ward? There was a lot of vulnerable prey in the hospital. It would be like setting off a bomb.

"I'm not crazy," she whispered.

Rylie was surprised to see Gwyn crying, too. She didn't think her aunt could cry. "I know, sweetheart," she said, hugging Rylie tight. "I know."

Fifteen

Truth

They admitted Rylie for the day. There wasn't anybody available to evaluate her until Monday, and after Gwyn's conversation with a doctor—during which she avoided using the word "werewolf"—they decided to keep her for observation.

"Observation" was a funny word, because it seemed to mean giving Rylie a room in the hospital and then ignoring her. They stuck her with a girl whose arms were bandaged from elbow to wrist. She refused to talk. That was fine with Rylie.

She was checked into the hospital in time for dinner, but their idea of food was a roll and reheated pasta with Jell-O. There was one little meatball on the plate that didn't taste like real meat. Gwyn went out to get a half dozen cheeseburgers and helped her by eating the buns and French fries while Rylie ate the patties.

"Thanks," she said. It was the only time she spoke to her aunt the entire time.

The nurses didn't make Gwyn leave after visiting hours ended, but there wasn't space in the room for her, so she slept between two chairs in the waiting room.

Rylie sat in bed with her knees to her chest, watching the seconds tick by on the clock and wondering what would happen in the morning. The girl with the bandaged arms was clicking through channels on the TV aimlessly for hours.

What if Rylie was crazy? It was likelier than being a werewolf. She never remembered being an animal anymore, so maybe she was losing her mind on the moons rather than transforming.

She might have preferred being crazy to being a monster, but that would have meant everything over the summer was a hallucination, too. Including Seth.

All she had to do to remind herself of the horrible truth was glance in the bathroom mirror. Her eyes used to be blue, and that shade of gold wasn't natural. The scars on her chest hadn't come from nowhere, either.

What would she tell the psychologist? They would think the werewolf thing was a nervous breakdown, too. She couldn't tell them the truth if she didn't want to be put in a straight jacket.

Of course, Eleanor couldn't get her in a psychiatric ward.

She managed to sleep fitfully for a couple hours in the early morning, but a nurse woke her up for breakfast. Rylie threw everything in the trash except the turkey bacon. The girl with the bandaged arms had vanished.

A few minutes later, they took her to be evaluated.

"I'll wait right out here," Gwyn said, squeezing Rylie's hand.

She made herself smile.

The therapist was a smiling middle-aged woman with a pen over one ear and perfect fingernails. The name plate on her desk said Rita Patterson. "Good morning," she greeted. "How are you feeling this morning?"

"I don't like hospitals," Rylie said.

"Why is that?"

"You don't go to a hospital for anything fun."

Rita had a rich, pleasant laugh. "Unfortunately, that's true. Now, I've been told your aunt brought you in because she's worried about you, so I have a little worksheet for you to fill out. It's how we assess your risk level."

She pushed a paper across the desk, and Rylie looked at the first question: *Do you have thoughts of self-harm?* It had boxes to check for "yes" or "no." All of the questions were similar.

"I'm not suicidal," Rylie said without touching a pen.

"No? Do you want to tell me why you came in yesterday?"

"I told Aunt Gwyneth that I'm a werewolf. She thought I went crazy."

"Are you a werewolf?" Rita asked.

It was kind of a weird question. She wasn't asking what Rylie thought. She asked if she really was a werewolf.

"Yes. I am."

The room was very quiet. Rylie thought her heart might be pounding loud enough for the therapist to hear it.

She had decided overnight that the best way to protect herself from Eleanor would be to get locked up. If she could get them to put her in a padded cell, she would be guarded all the time. They probably wouldn't keep her for very long, but it would be a few days of safety.

So Rylie would be honest. The truth was crazy enough without embellishment.

Rita took the pen from its position over her ear and tapped it against her lips. "How did you become a werewolf, Rylie?"

"I was bitten by another werewolf."

"And all of a sudden, you changed?"

"No," Rylie said. "I changed slowly. It took three months for me to become a werewolf." Her voice shook when she said it.

Slowly, very slowly, Rita set down her pen. She leaned forward to take the risk assessment paper from the desk, and Rylie noticed a glimmer of silver around her neck. The therapist was wearing a necklace with a five pointed star medallion.

Rita peered closely into Rylie's eyes.

"When did it happen?" she asked.

"Over the summer. I was bitten at Camp Silver Brook."

A strange expression flashed over the therapist's face, and then she sat back. She cleared her throat and typed a quick note on her computer.

"Well, Rylie," Rita said. She started writing on the risk assessment worksheet, and Rylie tilted her head to read it. She was filling it out for her. "Well, well. *Do* you have thoughts of self-harm?"

"Never."

"Do you ever think you would be better off dead?"

"No. I want to live. But I am a werewolf," she added, since the therapist didn't seem to be nearly as worried about that statement as Rylie expected. "I eat cows and stuff. Alive." Rita still didn't look surprised. "With my teeth." A little louder, she said, "When I'm an animal."

"I would be very careful who you say that to," Rita said in a low voice.

Surprise jolted through Rylie. "What?"

The therapist pushed a button on her desk, and a nurse opened the door, letting Gwyn into the room while Rylie was still gaping at Rita. Her aunt took the chair beside her.

"You are a perfectly normal girl," Rita said. "Stress gets to everyone sometimes. We don't always make the right decisions, but that doesn't mean there's anything wrong with us."

"But..." Rylie trailed off.

Did the therapist believe her? Did she already know?

"What do you think we should do with you?" Rita asked.

"Admit me to a psychiatric hospital," Rylie said. "Lock me up. I'm a danger to society."

Gwyn's jaw dropped. "Rylie—"

"I'm going to recommend that you see a therapist once a week. I know someone with an office in your town who sees patients on Friday afternoons." Rita took hospital stationary out of her desk and wrote down a phone number. "But I also know someone specializing in your kind of issues, Rylie. Someone who has handled a lot of young men and women just like you."

"What do you mean?"

"Scott Whyte is a psychologist in California. His expertise should allow him to give you the kind of intensive care you need."

"California?" Gwyn asked, voice sharp. "We can't fly her to California for regular treatment."

"Call him and see if you can make arrangements," Rita said, staring at Rylie as she said it. "Please." The star on her necklace seemed to attract light to it. "You don't need to be institutionalized, but you could certainly use some special attention."

Rita stood, and that was that. Rylie wasn't going to get locked up. She twisted her hands in dismay. "Are you sure I shouldn't be admitted?" she asked as the therapist walked them to her door. "What if I really am dangerous?"

"You're not, Rylie," Gwyn said. "Calm down."

"Watch out for yourself," Rita whispered when her aunt wasn't looking. "You and I both know it wouldn't be safe for you to be in a hospital for very long."

She opened her mouth to ask questions, but the door shut, Gwyn filled out some paperwork, and it was time to go home.

Rylie's mind whirled. Was it possible that other people knew about werewolves? What did that star mean? She stared at the two phone numbers Rita gave them and wondered what, exactly, Scott Whyte specialized in.

They didn't talk on the drive home. Her aunt's knuckles were white on the steering wheel, and the lines on her face looked deeper than they had before going to the hospital.

Rylie was afraid the Chevelle or the motorcycle would be parked outside the house when they got back to the ranch, but there was no sign anyone had been there. She took a shower and changed into jeans and a sweater. The weather had grown colder, and Gwyn was starting a fire in their woodstove.

She expected Gwyn to confront her about the werewolf story, but she pulled on her boots to go outside immediately. "Do you have any homework to finish?" she asked.

Rylie nodded. "I have a paper to write for English, and a project with Kathleen."

"Then I reckon you should get to work."

And just like that, they were supposed to be back to normal.

• ◯ •

Rylie couldn't relax knowing Eleanor was onto her secret. She kept expecting her to make another kidnap attempt. At least Abel had been obvious about stalking her—Eleanor was much sneakier, and a thousand times more frightening.

She dreamed of hands snatching at her hair and woke up on the floor more than once, having thrashed her way out of bed in the middle of violent dreams.

All she could think about was running away. She packed a bag with spare clothes and hid it under her bed so she could leave at a moment's notice, but Gwyneth never let her out of sight long enough to make a break for it.

In truth, Rylie felt better having her aunt nearby. As crazy as Eleanor was, she was pretty certain she wouldn't make another abduction attempt until she was alone. And since Abel wasn't coming in for work anymore, they had a lot more to do around the ranch.

"I wonder where he went," Gwyn said. "He hasn't shown up at all this week."

Rylie wondered how she would react if she knew her niece had bitten him. That might actually get her locked up this time. "I can call the newspaper and place another ad," she suggested.

"Yeah. We should probably do that."

Her sixteenth birthday came and passed. Gwyneth bought her a cake from the bakery in town and put Rylie's name on it with candles. As a present, she gave her a new diary with a leather cover and a gold ribbon.

"I remember you used to always be writing in one of these. I thought you might like a new one."

"Thank you," Rylie said. She had lost her last one at camp the night that Jericho attacked everyone and hadn't written in it since. The memory of it was painful. She wasn't sure she wanted to start a new journal.

"Have you thought more about going for a ride on Butch?" Gwyn asked. "He could sure use the exercise."

"I don't think I can."

"Suit yourself."

Her aunt didn't ask again.

Rylie saw Seth at school, but she avoided him so she wouldn't have to tell him what his mom had done. She wasn't sure how he would react.

Kathleen met her at the library during lunch, and they worked on their project together. At least, that was the official story—they couldn't seem to tolerate each other long enough to get anything done. They couldn't even pick a topic.

Their project was due in a week, but while most of the other groups had a rough draft, they were still stuck on the brainstorming phase. The worksheets the teacher had given them were still blank. And Rylie's patience had met its limit.

"That's a stupid idea!" Rylie snapped after Kathleen proposed the same topic for the sixth time. "I already told you, I don't want to do a project about that. Nobody cares about the settlers!"

Kathleen slammed her book shut. "Maybe you're just too stupid for history class."

She shoved her chair back and stood, snatching the books from the table. "I'll just write this stupid paper on my own!"

"Fine!"

Rylie stormed out of the library.

Eleanor was waiting in the parking lot.

She was in the driver's seat of Abel's Chevelle, and her stare was colder than the autumn breeze. Her hand was pressed against the glass like she wanted to reach through and grab Rylie again.

Rylie dropped the books in shock. They spilled across the sidewalk, and she dropped to her knees to grab them.

By the time she looked up, Eleanor was gone.

She spent the rest of the afternoon hiding in a locked bathroom stall. Every time the door opened, she thought it would be Seth's mom, but it was always another student.

"What's wrong?" Gwyn asked when she picked Rylie up that afternoon. "The way you're twitching, you look like you're getting attacked by flies."

"Nothing is wrong," she said, forcing a smile.

It didn't look like Gwyn believed her, but she wouldn't have believed the truth either, so Rylie kept smiling as they headed home. It made her cheeks hurt.

"I made you an appointment with a therapist." Gwyn handed her a slip of paper with a date and time on it.

"Is this the specialist?" Rylie asked.

"No, we don't have the money for that, and I'm sure you're not as bad as that Rita seemed to think. This one should be good enough. You'll start going once a week for a little while."

"Oh. Okay."

"That day is this Friday."

The day after the full moon. "Cool," Rylie said. She couldn't make herself sound grateful at all. "Thanks."

Gwyneth followed her inside when they got home. "We need to have a talk. You got a few minutes?"

"What is it?" she asked, dropping her knapsack by the door.

"I'm leaving for a couple of days. I meant to tell you awhile ago, but..."

"Leave? Why?"

"You know how there's some things I haven't told you about? Like why I didn't go to Brian's funeral? This is part of that."

"Does it have to do with my dad?" Rylie asked.

"Not at all. Look, I want you to trust me. I want you to feel like you can tell me anything—including the truth about what happened at summer camp. But you can't trust me until I trust you. I'm going to let you stay at home alone. You understand?"

She nodded slowly. "I think so."

"You need to go to school every day and come home like normal. You'll have to see if you can get a ride in with John Frank's kids—they're the farmers three miles up the road. The ranch hands have everything covered here, so don't worry about keeping everything running. Make sure to feed the chicks."

"Where are you going?"

"I'll tell you when I get back," Gwyn said. "You've got some stuff that's so awful you can't talk about it, and I do, too. I'm not ready to share. That's going to be a long, hard talk. Can I trust you?"

Rylie nodded. What else could she do? "Yes."

She helped her aunt get all the clothes off the line and fold them into suitcases. Rylie tried to keep up a conversation, but after seeing Eleanor, it was hard to think about anything else.

Once her aunt was gone, she would be alone and vulnerable. She was sure Eleanor would attack. She could feel the huntress drawing closer, like the jaws of a tiger were closing in on her throat.

Rylie couldn't be at the ranch when they came for her.

"Call Jessica if you need help, or ask Jorge if you need something small. We should have plenty of food. I'll be back on Saturday. It won't be long at all," Gwyn said, throwing her suitcases in the back of the truck.

"Okay." Rylie hugged her, and Gwyn felt thinner and more fragile than before. "I'll miss you."

She stood at the top of the hill and waved as her aunt's truck receded. Dread settled over her shoulders as it grew smaller in the distance.

As soon as she was gone, Rylie ran inside to get her bag.

Since she had already packed, there wasn't much to do but grab some food and a little cash. Money wouldn't be a problem in the long term. She had inherited plenty of money from her dad when he died. But she didn't have access to it yet, and she couldn't buy a bus ticket with stocks.

Whenever they went shopping, Gwyneth got a wad of bills out of her bedroom. She never used a credit card, so she had to keep cash somewhere in there.

Rylie stood with her hand over the doorknob to her aunt's room as she struggled with an internal debate. Gwyn had said she wasn't allowed in her room a hundred times. She didn't want to steal, either.

She would pay Gwyn back. She would just borrow it for now.

Rylie pushed the door open.

Her aunt's sheets were rumpled at the foot of the mattress. Clothes were piled in a hamper next to an old TV sitting on a dresser with its drawers open. Rylie hung by the door uncertainly. When she was a little girl, she used to take naps in Gwyn's bedroom, and she remembered it being clean and organized. What changed?

There was a desk under the window and a jewelry box on the bedside, half-hidden behind a bunch of pill bottles. Rylie guessed it would be in one of those places.

She snuck inside like she was intruding on Sunday mass and opened the jewelry box. Some of her late grandmother's necklaces and rings were nestled in the velvet lining. Gwyn said Rylie could have it all someday, so they were as good as hers, but she couldn't make herself take anything.

There wasn't any money hidden in the jewelry box, so she opened the small refrigerator next to Gwyn's bed and looked inside. It was populated with more bottles of medication. Rylie turned them over to look at the labels.

They had long, strange names Rylie couldn't pronounce, like "ritonavir" and "fosamprenavir." The description said they were antiretrovirals. She bit her bottom lip. Weren't those really strong drugs?

Wandering over to her aunt's desk, she found a bunch of mail she had never seen before. There were hospital bills and pamphlets about experimental treatments. A thick book was hidden underneath a bunch of envelopes, so Rylie slid them off to look at the cover.

Her heart plummeted. It was a book on living with HIV and AIDS.

The implications of all the different medications next to Gwyn's bed struck her, and Rylie got dizzy. She had to sit on the desk chair.

Her aunt was sick.

Really sick.

How could it be? She thought only guys got AIDS, but her aunt liked other women. But there was no other reason to have all those pills. Gwyneth must have left to go get the special treatment from the pamphlet.

Had sharing their food all this time put Rylie at risk? Could werewolves contract AIDS?

Was Gwyn going to die?

Rylie went through the papers one by one. Some of the more recent bills were dated for treatment around the time her dad had died. So that was why Gwyn hadn't made it to the funeral.

The numbers quoted on the bills made her head spin. She couldn't imagine how anyone could afford treatment like that. Gwyn's sudden urge to sell her big ranch in Colorado made sense—she must have needed the extra money to pay her bills.

Sliding open a drawer, Rylie found several rolls of bills wrapped with rubber bands. She ran her fingers over them.

She couldn't take any money. Gwyn needed it.

And Gwyneth needed her, too. Rylie was all the family she had left. Who would take care of her and the ranch if her sickness got worse?

Rylie's hand covered her mouth. Her eyes burned.

"Gwyn," she whispered to the wall.

Sixteen

Mother Dear

Seth showed up early for school the next day, just like he did every other day, and sat on the sign by the front lawn with his feet hanging over the edge.

He finished writing a paper that was due that day and gave it a quick scan in the light of the rising sun to make sure he caught every mistake. It was hard keeping up on assignments when his mom thought it was a waste of time.

Slowly, students began to arrive. He muffled a big yawn as he tracked them entering the building. Things had been tense at home for the last few days, so he hadn't been getting very much sleep.

Something changed with Eleanor. She took the thumbtacks off her map and rarely came home. When she did, she didn't speak to him, and the occasional words she exchanged with Abel were frosty. He was too afraid to ask what had changed.

Abel's condition kept getting worse. The bite on his shoulder hadn't healed immediately, which made Seth think he wouldn't turn into a werewolf, but it seemed like he was fighting a serious flu. He threw up at least three times a day, and he complained of being freezing even though he was always drenched in sweat.

Seth didn't know what to do. His dad might have known how to handle that kind of bite, but he hadn't left any information in his notes. He brought as much food to Abel as he could, but they were going to run out of money. None of them would be eating soon.

Tate's BMW pulled into the parking lot, jolting Seth back to reality. A girl with a shock of blond hair sat in the passenger's seat.

Rylie.

The two of them were laughing together, but Seth was too far away to hear what they were saying. She looked like she was having fun with him. Seth could barely control his irritation.

Normally, Rylie looked miserable hanging out with Tate, but something seemed to have happened between the two of them. They were hanging out even more than usual, and she smiled a lot more. Seth didn't like to admit it, but he kind of preferred it when Rylie looked unhappy. Not that he wanted Rylie to be miserable—he just didn't want her to have fun with other guys.

She had been avoiding him since the morning after the moon, too. Seth stuffed his binder into his backpack and threw it over his shoulder.

He wasn't going to put up with her silence anymore. He was going to find out what was wrong.

Seth dropped from his seat on the sign and walked behind them as they approached the school buildings. Tate nudged Rylie with his elbow, and she slapped him back playfully. Seth resisted the urge to punch him in the face.

She waved at Tate, and they went in separate directions. Tate went in the first building, and she headed for the next. Seth snuck up behind her and dragged her behind a bush.

Rylie's whole body went tense. A growl slipped from her before she realized who it was.

"Seth?" She glanced around them. "We shouldn't be talking. What if—?"

"Abel's sick. He's not going to spy on us."

"What about your mom?"

"She doesn't know. It's okay," Seth said. "Where have you been? I went by your house after the new moon and you were gone, and then you've been avoiding me all week."

"I had to… um, I went out of town."

"I've been worried about you."

Rylie scuffed her feet. "Sorry. Is something wrong?"

"No, I just—I mean, we haven't talked. I wanted to make sure you're okay. It's not like I was trying to stalk you," he said. She wouldn't look at him. Why was she acting so distant? "Are you okay?"

"Is there a reason I shouldn't be?"

"You got shot, Rylie."

Her hand dropped to her leg. "Oh. It healed fine. Thanks." Seth waited for her to say something else, but she was biting her thumbnail and kept peeking over the bush. "We shouldn't hang out where other people can see, and I have to get to class. Can we talk later?"

She didn't wait for his response before leaving their spot behind the bushes.

Seth hurried to catch up with her. "Talk to me," he insisted.

"We shouldn't talk in the open," she whispered.

"Come on, Rylie." He grabbed her shoulders, forcing her to stop. People were watching them, but he didn't care. "What's going on?"

Her eyes searched his face, and her gaze was like being under the weight of twin full moons. She reached up to touch his chin. It looked like she wanted to say something to him. He could practically see it hovering on her lips.

"Seth…" The bell rang. Her eyes dropped. "Never mind. I'll talk to you later."

She went into her class, leaving Seth alone in the quad.

He thought about Rylie all day. Her eyes had burned into his skull, and he kept seeing them when he looked at his notes instead of formulas and diagrams.

Rylie had always been excited to see Seth. He had come to expect her eagerness. He could show up whenever she wanted and she always made time for him. This new avoidance unsettled him.

His dad used to say that the spirit of the wolf ate the spirit of the man when they were bitten, which was why werewolves were evil. The changes they caused were so profound that the humans might as well have died on the night they were attacked. Seth had never known anyone before and after the bite, so he didn't know if that was true, but Rylie had definitely changed.

Something told Seth that wasn't the problem. Tate nudging Rylie and their shared laughter flashed through his mind. He clenched his fist, snapping his pencil in half.

"Seth?"

He realized it was the third time his name had been called. He looked up to find his chemistry teacher standing over him.

"What?" he asked.

Someone in the back of the room giggled.

"I asked if you'd solved the formula," said Ms. Lennon.

Seth looked at his paper, but he hadn't even written it down. "No. I didn't."

When the last bell of the day rang, he hurried to the parking lot hoping that he could give Rylie a ride home. He got outside just in time to see her disappearing with Tate again. His heart sank.

While Rylie avoided him, he had done some research into Tate's family. They were rich. Really rich. Seth's family didn't even have a couch, but Tate's parents had a summer home in Hawaii.

What if this didn't have anything at all to do with werewolves and hunting?

He brooded about it as he rode out on Abel's motorcycle. Seth meant to go home, but he looped around the small town three times before finally getting on the road out to the Gresham ranch.

There was no sign of Gwyneth's truck when he pulled up, and Tate's BMW was gone, too. Only Jorge's car was parked out back.

Seth parked and went looking for Rylie. The house was silent, so he checked the garden, and found it empty there too. A lot of the plants had shriveled from the recent frost.

He finally found her standing at the open door of the stables, watching the horses with a wrinkled nose.

"What are you looking at?" he asked, standing behind her.

Rylie glanced over her shoulder at him. "My aunt said I could get my driver's license if I rode one of the horses. She would even let me take myself to school with the truck."

"Sounds like a good deal."

"It is," she said, and her smile faded. "But I can't do it."

Seth almost asked her why, but then he remembered the first weeks after Abel had been bitten. He couldn't pass a dog without having it run in fear. Even if a werewolf looked like a normal person most of the time, animals could smell the difference. Abel got back to normal, but Rylie would probably spook horses.

"What are you going to do?" he asked.

"They can't smell me now, so they're being quiet. I bet I could sneak up on one of them. But as soon as they realized I was on their back..." She shivered. "What would you do if your mom found out about me?"

"That's not going to happen."

"But what if it did?" she insisted.

"I guess we would leave," Seth said. "You and me."

She didn't look as happy at the idea as he hoped. In fact, she actually looked sad. "Is that really the only good choice?"

"Unless you think dying is a good choice."

"Your mom scares me. She scares me more than I've been scared by anything before. She's way worse than Abel."

Seth took her hand. "Did something happen?"

"Nothing you need to worry about," she said.

All of a sudden, she flung her arms around him and squeezed tight. It was like being crushed by a giant vice. His ribs creaked. "Rylie…"

"Sorry." She eased up, but didn't let go. He wrapped his arms around her too. She was really warm. He knew it shouldn't feel nice to hold a werewolf, but he thought he could have stayed there for days if they had the time.

"What's wrong?" he asked.

"My aunt is sick," Rylie mumbled into his chest. "Really sick."

"You mean, like cancer sick?"

"Kind of."

"Is she going to die?"

She sniffled. "I don't know."

Seth tried to imagine what it would feel like if he found out his mom might die. Dad's death was sudden, but it wasn't surprising. It was part of a hunter's reality. He couldn't imagine anything tough enough to take out Eleanor.

"I'm sorry," he said. The wind came up, and he rubbed Rylie's back to try to keep her warm. The horses caught a sniff of her and started shifting in their stalls. "It's cold. Let's go in the house."

It wasn't much warmer inside. While Rylie started a fire in their woodstove, Seth explored a little. There were lots of boring knickknacks on their shelves, like novelty cats with clocks in their stomachs, but he discovered photo albums under the coffee table.

He opened the first one. The first picture had a younger, blond-haired Gwyneth with a grinning toddler in her lap. The man behind them looked like he hated to be photographed.

Seth's mom only had one picture of him and his brother as children. It was a photo of them standing over Abel's first kill.

"That's me and Gwyn with my dad," Rylie said, peering over his shoulder. "I miss him so much sometimes."

"Only sometimes?"

"I don't think he would have liked me as a werewolf."

He shut the cover. "We should probably talk about the full moon tomorrow."

"Why?" she asked, sitting next to him on the couch.

"It falls on Samhain. This moon is kind of special."

"What's Sow-in?"

"All Hallows' Eve," he explained. "It's a holiday for witches. My dad used to say that werewolves were the worst on Halloween, but I don't know if that's true. I think he used to make up a lot about werewolves. But if he was right, I don't think I can control you."

"Oh. I forgot about Halloween. I don't even have a costume." She smiled a little, but it was a sad smile. "I bet I could win the contest at school tomorrow if I showed up furry."

"Not if you eat the judges."

Rylie didn't laugh. "So what will we do? Where should I hide?"

"We can't go back to the mine in case my mom checks it. Your aunt has a cellar, doesn't she? We could try that." Seth took a deep breath. "If you are as bad as my dad said you would be, I don't know if I can control you. We should probably use the muzzle, and maybe some wolfsbane."

"Isn't that poisonous to me?" she asked.

"Yeah. A small dose would only knock you out, though. You wouldn't feel much pain."

Rylie rested her head on his shoulder and he pulled her close to him. They watched the fire as it grew dark outside.

"Stay with me," she said. "Here. At the ranch. You don't need to live with your family if you don't want to."

"I can't do that, Rylie," he said. "Abel's sick. He needs me. I don't think your aunt would be happy to find out I moved in, either."

"She's not in town. I'll make something up when she gets back. Please? I would feel a lot better if you were here. I'm scared on my own." Her eyes pleaded with him. Seth wanted to say yes. He really did.

"I won't let anything happen to you. I promise. Nobody will hurt you."

"Will you spend the night here with me? Just for tonight?"

"What about Tate?" Seth asked.

Rylie leaned back to look at him. "Huh? What about Tate?"

"I thought you guys were dating now," he said. "You've been with him a lot."

"Dating? Are you serious? He's like… I don't know what he's like. But it's not like that between us. We're really good friends. That's all."

Seth probably shouldn't have been so happy to hear that news. "Okay, I'll stay tonight and tomorrow."

"Thank you," she whispered.

•〇•

Eleanor was waiting for Seth when he came home.

She could practically smell the werewolf on him. It pained her to wait for another attack, but the beast surprised her. Eleanor hadn't expected it to escape. She didn't want to chase Rylie down again—it would be much easier to wait until she turned so she could shoot her.

So Eleanor waited. Watching her son trailing after the werewolf like a lovesick puppy was nauseating. And when he came home with a dumb smile, it was all she could do not to slap those stupid thoughts out of his thick head.

As soon as Seth came home, he went into the bedroom to check on his brother. Eleanor hung by the door to watch them.

Abel was sleeping again. It was almost like he had gone into hibernation after the last moon. He didn't stir from his sleep until Seth lifted the corner of the bandage on his shoulder.

"What do you think, doc?" Abel asked, his voice ragged with sleep.

"Looks like you're going to survive. That's too bad. I want your car," Seth said.

Abel laughed. "You're a jerk."

"And you're ugly."

"Go run yourself off a bridge," his brother mumbled, rolling over to go back to sleep.

Seth stood, and his smile faltered when he saw Eleanor watching. It came right back after a moment. He was trying to deceive her with his every motion.

"How was school today?" she asked.

"It was fine."

He shut Abel's door and moved around the trailer, digging through the fresh laundry he had cleaned at the Laundromat the day before. He picked out a shirt and pants and stuffed them in his backpack.

"What are you doing?"

"I'm going to camp out in the hills tonight," Seth said. It would have been more convincing if he'd met her eyes while he was lying. "I'm going to look for places the werewolf might make a den."

He was going to spend the night with that *thing*. "No, Seth," Eleanor said. "I don't think so."

Uncertainty flicked through his eyes. "Why?"

So he was going to play innocent? Eleanor couldn't imagine how such an arrogant little jerk could have come from her womb. He was nothing like Jim.

She blocked the door with her body so he couldn't leave. Seth probably could have overpowered her. He was shorter, but much stronger. The impudence in his expression made her so angry that she could have spit on him.

"You tell me why."

"Good question, Mom," Seth said. "You never cared where I went before now."

"That's because you weren't sneaking around with some blond tramp before."

All the color vanished from his face.

"Mom—"

She grabbed his chin in her hand, digging her fingernails into his jaw. "A werewolf. A *demon*. One of those killed your daddy and mauled your brother, and you're fooling around with it." She drew in a long, shaking breath and dropped her hand. There were four perfect crescents in his skin. "This is some... some kind of teenage rebellion. You've had a hard time dealing with your destiny, but you're young. You can't see the big picture."

"Let me explain," he said, holding up his hands. She couldn't control her anger any longer.

Eleanor slapped him. It rang out in the trailer, and the silence that followed the crack was deep and heavy. Seth's hand flew to his face.

"I'll do all the explaining this time, and you'll keep your nasty little mouth shut," she hissed through clenched teeth. "Your brother's ripping himself apart because that thing tore his shoulder open, so I don't care how you've rationalized all this. The only relationship you're going to have with that werewolf from here on out is at the end of a gun. If you got a problem with that, then—then—" Eleanor's fists shook. "Well, I don't give half a damn if you've got a problem with it, boy."

"You can't make me stay,' Seth said.

Eleanor drew her pistol from the small of her back, and his eyes went wide. She pressed it into his sternum.

"I can't?"

"Mom, what are you—?"

"Sit down."

The gun made him awfully obedient. Seth lowered himself to the floor of the trailer. She grabbed the ropes without dropping her aim. These were the only ones she had left—that werewolf had destroyed the other ones. They might not have been strong enough for a monster, but they would be strong enough for her so-called son.

"Don't do this," he said, eyes round. "Mom. Please."

"I can't trust you anymore." She gave a harsh laugh. "Jim would be so disappointed."

He opened his mouth to speak, but Eleanor didn't care what he had to say anymore.

She whipped the gun across his face, and he collapsed.

Seventeen

All Hallows

Seth didn't come back to Rylie's house that night, and he wasn't at school when she arrived the next morning. She stood under the tree and watched for the motorcycle until the second bell rang.

Something had happened. Something was wrong.

Even worse, she could feel the moon even though the sun had just risen for the day. The wolf was already stirring inside of her. Her skin prickled as though it was covered in fur, and she had to run her hands down her skin to make sure she was still human.

"Seth," she whispered. "Where are you?"

The only response was the rustling of dry leaves as they blew past on the sidewalk.

Rylie found her desk in homeroom by instinct instead of eyesight. It was the day the school celebrated Halloween, so most of the kids were wearing costumes. Their faces were covered in leering death masks and cloaks, and every other mouth was fanged. They laughed shrilly and shrieked instead of speaking. The noise drove into her skull like steel spikes.

The teacher didn't try to make them read. He passed out candy and let everyone sit on their desks talking. Rylie pulled out her cell phone and watched the screen, hoping Seth would call her.

Maybe nothing was wrong. Maybe he'd been sidetracked by something else.

But her phone stayed silent.

Her second class was decorated with paper skeletons and red streamers. They watched a movie about witches while eating popcorn balls, but Rylie refused to take hers. Corn sounded disgusting. She craved something bloody and squirming.

Kathleen and Rylie were scheduled to present their paper in third period.

"Did you write it?" she whispered when Rylie sat next to her. Kathleen was dressed like a fairy with wings made of filmy cloth, but the short skirt made her look like a dumpy stripper.

Rylie tried to focus on her partner's lips, but she couldn't make sense of the words. "Write what?"

"Oh no," Kathleen said. "You didn't write it. Oh no. We're so screwed." She turned into a flurry of motion, opening her binder and throwing around papers. Hysterics made her sweat smell like adrenaline.

Rylie savored the scent.

Panicked prey were the best. They never saw the end coming.

There was another smell, too, beyond the wafting odor of panic, buttered popcorn, and candy corn. Something... bloody.

Rylie stood up, ignoring Ms. Reedy as she repeated her name. She wandered into the hall. It was empty during class, but streamers fluttered in the breeze made by the heater.

Meat. Rylie smelled meat.

She stepped out the doors to the quad and her foot connected with something soft. It was a package wrapped in butcher's paper. Rylie knelt to untie it, and her mouth watered at the sight of a raw cut of lamb.

There was a note beside it in unfamiliar handwriting: *Your last meal.*

Rylie clutched the paper as she searched the quad with her eyes. Somehow, she knew it was Eleanor's handwriting. She was watching.

"What is that?"

She spun. Kathleen stood behind her with her nose wrinkled. Her mouth fell open when she saw Rylie's bloody hands.

Frightened prey. Delicious.

Rylie shut her eyes so she didn't have to see the pulse throbbing in Kathleen's throat. "Go away."

"Ms. Reedy says you need to come back to class."

"Get out of here. Go!"

Kathleen ran into the classroom. Rylie's stomach growled.

She ran her fingers over the cut of lamb, digging her fingernails into it. She was so hungry. The human side of her was shrieking with alarm—*Eleanor left it, don't eat that, it's a trap!*—but it was a small voice fading into the background.

She shouldn't eat a piece of meat she found on the ground. It was insane. It was animal.

It was... irresistible.

Rylie lifted the meat to her mouth and sank her teeth into it.

She jerked back and dropped the lamb. It made a *splat* against the cement. Rylie spat, trying to clear her mouth of the sour tang that filled her mouth.

Silver. Eleanor injected the meat with silver.

She heard footsteps approaching and realized she would have blood all over her face. She couldn't let anyone see her. Rylie jumped over the package, forcing herself to walk away from the sweet smell of food, and hurried to the bathroom.

Scrubbing her hands and face, she watched the lamb's blood circle the drain.

Your last meal.

It hadn't been a serious attempt to kill her... yet. It was a message.

Eleanor was coming for her.

The bathroom door opened, and Dean Black entered holding the juicy cut of lamb away from her body like it was a bomb. Rylie checked her reflection to make sure she was clean before straightening.

"What is this?" the dean asked.

Rylie peered over the butcher's paper like she hadn't seen the package before. It wasn't hard to make herself look sickened. Now that she had picked up the taste of silver, she could smell it in the back of her throat.

"Gross. Where did you find that?"

"Don't play games with me. I saw you putting this outside your classroom. Is it some kind of sick Halloween prank?"

"I didn't put it there," Rylie said.

"You need to come to the office with me, Miss Gresham."

She recoiled. "Why? I told you I didn't put it there!"

"I've heard that a thousand times before. Scoot. We're going to call your guardian."

The wolf bristled. Who did this woman think she was, trying to push her around? Nobody could tell Rylie what to do.

She stalked over to the dean and slapped the lamb out of her hands. It splattered all over the floor. The dean shrieked and jumped back, but it was too late. Blood splashed on her pumps.

Dean Block stared at it numbly, and Rylie took the opportunity to push past her toward the door.

The dean caught her arm. "I don't think so. You've gone too far this time. You're—"

Rylie's hand clamped down on Dean Block's wrist, and she pinned her against the wall without any effort. The older woman struggled. She could barely move in the iron grip of the wolf.

"I said I didn't do it," Rylie growled. "I'm not going anywhere with you. Got it?"

She didn't realize how hard she had been holding onto the dean until she let go and the woman sprawled across the floor. Dean Block's hand landed on the lamb and slipped. Her head bounced against the linoleum.

The shout of surprise went right to Rylie's stomach. Her heart pounded. She felt dizzy.

There was blood everywhere. It smelled amazing.

Humans were even better than lamb.

"No," Rylie whispered.

She fled the bathroom before Dean Block could collect herself. When she hit the quad, she kept running.

Rylie was going to get in trouble this time. A *lot* of trouble. Throwing the book had been one thing, but pushing the dean meant a call to the police. She couldn't get taken into custody. She would transform and kill everyone.

She ran through town blindly, propelled by the wolf's hunger. The smell of blood had driven her to the edge of starvation. She needed to eat something. *Anything.*

The sun was high in the sky, burning through her body even though the air was chilly. Running was hard on two legs. She wanted to drop to all fours and flee into the forest. The wolf longed for freezing rivers and pine trees, for cold stone and warm earth.

But most of all, she longed to sink her teeth into something hot and alive.

She ran past a house with a dog in the front yard. It leaped at her, barking wildly.

Rylie stopped dead on the sidewalk.

It was a little thing with short yellow fur. A Chihuahua, she thought, even though she didn't know much about dogs. It bared its teeth and barked like it was ten times bigger.

She reached over the fence and grabbed it by the neck. Small jaws snapped at her as it thrashed like a tiny, furious demon.

No. This is wrong…

Her human side was growing fainter every second.

Giving it a hard shake made the dog yelp. She could snap its neck so easily and tear into its soft belly. She could—

"Hey! Get your hands off my dog!"

A fat woman burst through the front door of the house, pulling her pants up as she rushed down the sidewalk. The dog twisted and sunk its teeth into Rylie's wrist. Shocked, she dropped it to the ground.

"What are you doing, you sick freak? Get away from my house!" The woman ripped a lawn decoration out of her yard and brandished the spiked end at her. "I'll call the police!" She shoved the gate open, letting the Chihuahua dart into the yard again.

Rylie ducked beneath the swinging spike, and then she shoved.

The huge woman flew through the air. Her back crashed into the white picket fence. She screamed and screamed and *screamed.*

So hungry.

Sirens wailed in the distance. Someone must have called for help.

The noise scared Rylie enough that she broke into a run again, and this time, Rylie didn't let herself stop for anything.

The world was a blur of sound and scent and sirens. Cars blew past her. She ran between two houses and climbed a fence into a farm. Stalks of corn ripped at her as she blasted through the fields.

When she reached the end of her aunt's property, she let herself collapse. Her skin was going to rip itself off her body.

She screamed and tore at her hair.

Hungry.

Her stomach turned inside out. The wolf was consuming her. She could feel its teeth scraping against her ribs and its claws digging into her gut.

Something was moving in the field.

Goats.

Her gaze sharpened on them. The flock pressed themselves into a corner, bleating pathetically.

It was too much. She couldn't control herself anymore.

Rylie lunged.

The flock scattered, but she was faster than they were, and her clawed hands fell upon a small goat near the back. She pinned it to the earth and buried her teeth in its throat.

Hot blood exploded across her tongue. It spurted with every beat of the goat's slowing heart. Its helpless cries became strangled as little hooves kicked at the air. The musky fur tasted like dirt, but the meat was so juicy on her tongue.

Ripping her head away, she grabbed the head of the goat and twisted. It snapped. Then it didn't make noise at all.

Rylie dug in. It was like the first breath of air after being drowned in the ocean. The relief of having food—*real* food— made her relax instantly. Every bite was more delicious than the last.

When she threw the goat aside, it didn't look like an animal anymore.

And she was still hungry.

The wolf attacked the goats one after another. She ripped out their throats and feasted on their flesh. It was never enough. The more she devoured, the hungrier she became.

When she finished tearing into her fifth goat, Rylie let its carcass fall and sat back on her haunches. She licked her fingers, savoring the tastes lingering on her tongue.

The sun was dropping. The moon's pull was rising.

But Rylie was already gone.

Footsteps.

"My son thinks you're different," said a woman's voice. "If only he were here to see how wrong he is."

The wolf spun too late.

Eleanor aimed a gun at her. She tried to remember human words so she could protest, but she didn't get a chance.

The pistol fired with a thunderous crack.

Eighteen

The Choice

"Wake up. I've got a present for you."

Sleep peeled away from Seth slowly. It was like trying to pull himself out of a pit of quicksand. But when he saw his mother's face over his, with a knife in her hand, he came to his senses with a shock.

He tried to jerk away from her, but there was nowhere to go. She had tied his wrists and ankles behind his back. His limbs were completely numb.

Seth was in the same place he had spent the night—the storage space beneath their mobile home. He spent all day struggling to get free by rubbing the ropes against the edge of a wooden post, but he hadn't gotten anywhere. Spiders had been crawling on him for hours.

Somehow, the worst part wasn't being hogtied by Eleanor and shoved under the dark floor of a trailer. It wasn't having a wolf spider spend half the night on his cheek, either. The worst part was imagining what his mom might do to Rylie while he was bound.

"Mom," he growled. It came out sounding like an insult.

She rolled him over and sliced the ropes off his wrists. Sensation began returning with electric jolts, and he groaned, rubbing at his arms.

"Can you move?" she asked. He nodded. It was only a half-truth. When he tried to wiggle his toes, tingling pain shot through his whole body. But admitting he would be slow to move seemed like a terrible idea when his mother had a silver knife the length of his forearm. "Good. I have something to show you."

She crept out of the crawlspace, and Seth followed. "I thought I was in trouble."

"Oh, you are. But you've got a chance to make it better."

Night had fallen again. Seth felt total disorientation. It had been night when his mom threw him beneath the trailer, but even though he lost track of the time, he was sure it must have been at least a day since their confrontation. It couldn't be the same night, could it?

"What time is it?" he asked

"Just after sunset."

He heard a thumping from the bedroom. "What is that?"

"Abel. He's bad tonight," she said.

"Is he going to change?"

"No, but he hurts like hell. The moon's really beating him tonight." Eleanor's lip curled. "You have that *thing* to thank for it." Seth moved for the door to check on him, but her fingers bit into his shoulder. "We can't do anything for him. We've got something else to do tonight."

She pulled him outside. The moon filled the sky. He realized with a shudder that Rylie must have changed. Had she gotten somewhere safe for the transformation?

"Where are we going?" he asked.

"You'll see. Get in the car."

They got into the Chevelle. It looked like half of their guns had been put in the backseat.

"I'm not going to hunt tonight," he said as Eleanor drove into the night.

"You won't have to."

He wasn't surprised when they pulled up to the Gresham ranch and parked behind the barn. Seth jumped out of the car, and he heard his mom's footsteps behind him as he moved for the house.

A silver shape emerged in the darkness. It was hard to make out at first, but as he got closer, Seth realized it was a cage. The bars were made of silver-laced iron. They used it to trap werewolves.

And there was a huge, golden-furred form inside it.

"Rylie!" he shouted, but Eleanor moved in his way.

"Don't even think about it," she said, clenching his shirt in her fist. "I gave birth to you, Seth. I raised you. Your daddy and I trained you to be a warrior for God against evil. Your affair with this… thing… is treason against your own blood."

He couldn't tear his eyes from Rylie. She thrashed against the bars. Every time she touched the iron, she jerked back again with a shrill cry. Her entire body seized. Eleanor had scattered wolfsbane across the ground, too, so there was nowhere safe for her to go.

Blood bubbled out of a bullet wound on her shoulder. Eleanor had already shot her.

Rylie would tear herself apart if she wasn't poisoned first.

"You're torturing her," Seth said.

"I saved her for you."

Cold shocked through him. "What?"

Eleanor handed one of the rifles to him. The metal was cold and heavy in his hands.

"This thing tried to kill her. She would kill you if she had the chance. You're going to shoot her and prove you're not as much of a waste as I think you are."

Rylie gave a long, agonized howl.

Seth's heart ached for her. Death would have been a mercy. Even if she survived, she would be in misery for weeks. The silver poisoning would be severe.

He stepped forward. Eleanor didn't stop him.

The wolf whined as he pointed the muzzle of his rifle through the bars.

"Do it already, Seth," she snapped. "I will if you won't."

He could save her from the pain.

Rylie grew weaker. She jumped at the bars one last time, rattling the entire cage, and then she collapsed. Her flesh sizzled. The pain must have been intense, but she didn't twitch.

She was slipping away from him, dying as he watched.

He knelt. "Are you there?" he whispered, but she didn't react. Her tongue lolled out of her mouth. She was drooling blood.

"Shoot her!"

No more. He couldn't watch for another second.

"I'm sorry, Rylie."

Seth fired.

The wolf shrieked...

...and the bullet smacked into the lock, shattering the metal. The latch swung open. The silence that followed was only broken by Rylie's whimpering.

Eleanor immediately raised her gun, and he saw her finger tense on the trigger. He whirled to aim the rifle at her. "Don't move," he said.

"Put it down, you dumb little shit. I'll kill her."

"And I'll kill you," he said, voice shaking.

Seth was sure that Eleanor would pull the trigger, and then he would have to pull his trigger too. He had never taken the time to imagine such a situation. Did his skill match his mother's? Was he strong enough, fast enough, to survive against her?

Could he really kill her?

Eleanor's lips trembled with fury. "You wouldn't."

Seth moved in front of her gun. She couldn't fire on Rylie without hitting him.

"Try me," he said. Something in his face must have convinced her that he was serious. She slowly set her gun on the ground. "Step back."

She didn't move. "Seth…"

"I told you to step back!"

In one smooth motion, she picked the gun up again, aimed it at Seth, and squeezed the trigger.

He moved an instant before she did.

Seth threw himself at her, knocking them both to the ground. The shot exploded in his ear and went wild.

They wrestled. Her elbow connected with his face. He smacked the heel of his palm into her nose and blood splattered down her lip.

He yanked the pistol out of her hands and leaped back, leaving her defenseless on the ground.

"What are you doing?" she asked, voice dangerously low.

"This is wrong. Can't you see? That's not a monster in there. That's Rylie! She's a human being! She has an aunt who loves her, and she likes sundresses and modern art, and—"

"And she's a *monster*," Eleanor spat.

"I love her, Mom."

She laughed. It was a hysterical laugh, the kind of cackle that came from a madman being wheeled into an asylum. "You love that thing? You *love* it? You know how I found her today? Look around the garden! See those dead goats? Those weren't coyotes—those weren't even killed by a wolf. They were slaughtered by that thing you *love* as a human, with her bare teeth."

He opened the cage with his free hand and grabbed a fistful of Rylie's fur, hauling her into the open. Her breathing was rapid and shallow. Her eyes were only half open.

"They were just goats," he said. He never dropped his aim.

SM Reine

"*Just goats?* It's *just goats* now—but isn't it always? It'll be humans next! Jim would be *furious!*"

"Dad's dead," Seth said.

"Because one of them murdered him and ate his liver!"

"After he murdered her entire pack!" Seth ran his hand down Rylie's side, ruffling her fur. She didn't respond. He turned to give Eleanor his full attention, putting both hands on the gun to steady it. "We've been on his vendetta for years. We're not a family. We're an army! Haven't you ever thought about what we're doing?"

She opened her mouth to argue—but then her gaze focused over his shoulder. "Look out!"

He was shocked to see Rylie climbing to her paws. Her entire body shook. Her fur was matted with sweat and blood, and he could see lesions on her nose where the bars had burned her skin.

Eleanor drew her knife, but Seth threw an arm out to stop her.

"Wait!"

The wolf staggered forward one step at a time. She was dripping blood from her jaws. Eleanor hadn't just thrown her in a cage. She had beaten her first, and now Rylie had internal injuries.

A low growl rose in her throat as Seth reached a hand for her. "Don't be suicidal. Injured wolves are very, very dangerous," Eleanor said, inching backward on the ground.

"She won't hurt me." He stepped forward and Rylie bared bloody teeth. He froze. "Rylie... it's me."

She whined.

He lowered to his knees and set the pistol on the ground, careful not to make any sudden motions.

"It will kill you," Eleanor said.

"Come on, Rylie," he whispered, tuning her out. "It's okay."

She twitched. It looked like silver poisoning might have advanced to the point of causing nerve damage. Her ear flicked back, and her right eye wouldn't open all the way.

His mom was right. Approaching a werewolf under the best of circumstances was dangerous, but trying to get close to one when she was injured and irrational was asking to get bitten.

But Seth knew she was different. He believed it with every fiber of his soul.

She loved him. She would never hurt him.

The wolf limped forward. Slowly, so slowly, she stretched out her head... and bumped her nose into his hand. It left a red smear on his palm.

"Lord in Heaven," Eleanor murmured.

And then Rylie collapsed.

Her full weight fell against his legs, and he almost fell because she was so big. It wasn't an attack. She went completely limp with her eyes rolled into the back of her head.

"Rylie?" he asked, touching the ruff of fur around her neck.

His hand came away soaked with blood.

No.

Werewolves were almost impossibly hard to kill. Seth had seen Abel plant a silver bullet in the skull of a werewolf four years ago, and it dragged itself away to survive. They had to wait two weeks to kill it.

So Rylie couldn't be dead.

She *couldn't* be.

Seth pushed his hand through her fur, searching for a heartbeat. He couldn't find anything.

"Rylie?"

Eleanor crawled over and touched his shoulder. "She's gone, boy. You should—"

He shoved her off of him. "Don't touch me! Go to the car. Get bandages. Get... I don't know, just go get *something*. She might change back in the morning. She's not dead!"

"We don't have bandages."

Seth didn't hear her. He ran his hand through her fur, pressed his hands to her ribs, and shut his eyes. He needed to feel a breath. Just one breath, and he knew she would be fine.

"Go away," he said. "Leave us alone."

"After everything you've done? You little—"

Seth grabbed his mom by the throat, and he felt gripped by a fury so inhuman that for one instant, he thought he was the werewolf instead of Rylie. Eleanor gurgled. "Go," he said, and his voice was thick with grief.

He shoved her back. She sprawled out on the ground.

"I hope you're happy with your little bitch," she said. "My blessings for a happy life together—however long that is."

Eleanor left, but Seth barely noticed or cared.

He drew his knife and found the bullet wound on Rylie's shoulder. She wouldn't heal with silver inside of her. Digging out bullet fragments with the tweezers had nearly blinded her with pain, but he didn't have time to be gentle now.

"I'm sorry," he whispered. "This would hurt if you were awake."

He cut the bullet wound open wider and reached in with his first finger and thumb. She didn't move. Seth dug around until he found the bullet flattened against her shoulder blade, which felt like it had cracked from the impact.

Seth flung the silver into the night and felt her nose again. Her breaths were so slow and faint that he wasn't sure if he was imagining them.

He struggled to lift her body, but he had to get away from the cage. They made it as far as the tree before his strength gave out.

Seth had promised to spend the night with Rylie. He had sworn to protect her.

I'm scared, she had said. *Stay with me.*

"I'm not going anywhere," he said to the wolf in his lap.

She didn't respond.

Nineteen

Sunrise

When the golden line of dawn broke over the horizon, Seth had his back leaned against the tree with Rylie's body pressed against his legs. He watched the sky as it brightened without moving.

He felt like a dried out husk. It was like he left his body sometime in the middle of the night, and now he watched everything from a great distance.

Seth clung to the hope that the sun would turn Rylie back like a prayer. But the longer he sat with her, the less he thought it was likely. His insides felt weighted with lead. "Rylie," he whispered into the chill morning air. His breath curled out of him in foggy lines.

The sun inched up the hill and touched his fingers where they rested in her fur.

Her side jerked. She sucked in a long breath.

He sat up to watch as her skin rippled. The fur rolled along her body like a wave passing through her.

And then... she changed.

The golden fur slipped from her skin as her tail shrunk back into her body. Paw pads lengthened into fingers and toes. Her nose receded into her face, and the sharp fangs shrank into human canines.

It only took a few moments for Rylie to become human again. She was dirty, but completely uninjured and whole.

Her eyes opened and focused on him. They glimmered with tears. "Seth?"

He couldn't respond. If he spoke, he would lose control of himself, and he never cried. Seth wrapped his arms round her back and held her tight to his body, burying his face in her hair.

They held onto each other until the whole farm was bathed in golden sunlight. Seth realized she was shivering and took off his jacket to wrap it around her, but Rylie didn't want to let go of him long enough to get it on her arms.

"Seth," she said, clinging to his shoulders, "your dad was right. It was horrible. My mind… I changed before the moon. I almost killed a dog. I ate a bunch of goats! It was—"

He interrupted her. "Hey, hey, don't worry about it. They were goats. Nobody got hurt. You're okay."

"But I got mad at Dean Block. I pushed her. I'm going to be suspended from school!"

Eleanor had almost killed Rylie, and she was worried about *school*. Seth had to laugh. "Who cares? You can finish high school somewhere else."

She looked down at her bloody body. "What happened?"

Seth didn't know what to say. It was probably better if she didn't know what Eleanor had done.

"Nothing," he said. "Nothing important."

Their faces were so close together that he couldn't see anything else. Rylie didn't look anything like the girl he glimpsed on that first full moon so many months before. She looked like the spirit of a wild animal with her hair blowing behind her. It was simultaneously inhuman and intoxicating.

Seth didn't want to fight it anymore. He kissed her.

It wasn't like their first kiss when Jericho attacked the summer camp, which had been brief and hurried. His lips fell on hers, and they both paused—waiting, probably, to see if one of them would draw back. She reached up and laid her fingers on the back of his neck.

That small gesture was enough. His lips parted, and then they were kissing, really kissing. She tasted like blood. He didn't care.

When they parted, she was smiling. He smiled back.

A voice spoke from behind them. "So that's how it is."

Eleanor.

Seth moved to conceal Rylie, but his mom lifted her hands in the universal gesture of peace.

She looked terrible. It was like she had aged a decade overnight. Deep lines scored the sides of her mouth and between her eyebrows. He couldn't see a gun, but that didn't mean it wasn't there.

"What do you want?" Rylie growled.

"This isn't worth it, Seth," Eleanor said. "Let's go. We'll leave her alone. That's what you want, isn't it?" She looked defeated. He had never seen his mother like that.

"Where's Abel?"

"He's packing," she said stiffly.

"For what?"

"He says…" She cleared his throat. "He doesn't like what I've done. He thinks it's time to go out on his own. So it's time for you and me to go."

She thought Seth would go with her? The idea was ridiculous. He might have been seventeen, but he wasn't an idiot.

"Would you have shot me?" Seth asked.

A muscle in her jaw twitched. "You're my baby. I would never shoot you." He couldn't tell if she was lying or not.

"I'm not going with you. I'm done fighting Dad's battles."

She stiffened. "You're still a kid."

"I'll live with Abel."

"Seth—"

"I'm going to finish school, Mom. I'm going to graduate, and then I'm going to college. And I'm going to do it without you."

Eleanor looked tempted to kidnap him again. Her fists clenched and unclenched. Her barely-bridled fury boiled beneath the surface, and Seth braced himself for a fight.

Rylie got to her feet, hugging Seth's jacket around her. Even though she was a couple inches shorter than him, it barely covered enough to be decent. "You heard Seth," she said. "Go away. We don't want to see you again."

His mother's lip curled. "This is your fault."

"You're stupid if you think that's true."

Eleanor raised her hand, but Rylie didn't flinch.

"I can do better than to waste my time with you anyway," she said. And that was goodbye. She marched down the hill and waited by the Chevelle for a moment as though she expected Seth to change his mind and join her.

He didn't. He wrapped his arm around Rylie's shoulders and watched as it drove away.

"What am I going to do?" Seth asked.

She gripped his hand. "I said you could stay with me. My aunt's coming back today. I'll ask her. I mean, you're turning eighteen soon, right? So it would only be for a few months anyway."

"I can probably stay with Abel. That's not what I'm worried about. But…" Admitting the problem pained him. Seth grimaced. "We've never had much money. Without Dad's life insurance, I won't have anything at all."

"That's okay," Rylie said. "I could—"

"I don't want your money."

Her cheeks colored. "That's not what I was going to say. I could ask my aunt if you could work here, too, since we'll need a lot of help around the ranch if she's sick. She pays pretty good."

"Oh. Do you think she would hire me?"

"I'm sure she would. Gwyn trusts me," Rylie said firmly. She looked down at herself, and her cheeks got pinker. "Um… do you think we could go inside? I'm kind of freezing."

Seth laughed. "Yeah. Let's go."

•◯•

The wolf was unusually quiet after the moon on All Hallows' Eve. Rylie didn't feel the slightest bit of a stir as she went through her morning chores, and she even managed to feed the chicks without sending them into a panic.

She never felt too much the morning after a transformation, but now it was like she was hollow on the inside. The wolf wasn't just quiet. It had completely gone away.

"Do you think this is it for now?" she asked, standing by the pond with her shoulder bumping against Seth's.

"What?"

"The werewolf thing. I don't feel it at all."

He tangled his fingers with hers. "You're not cured, if that's what you're asking."

"But that was the worst it will get, right? I'll never have a day as bad as this Halloween."

"No. Probably not."

"Good," she said. "Then I want to try something."

Gwyn came home that afternoon to find them in the stables. Her aunt took one look at Seth, who was brushing and saddling Butch, and her eyebrows lifted so high on her forehead that they looked like they might fly off completely.

"Did you have fun while I was gone?" she asked. She looked exhausted. Her sleeves were rolled down to the wrists, but Rylie could see bruises on the backs of her hands.

"Not really. I missed you," Rylie said honestly.

Gwyn lowered her voice so Seth wouldn't be able to hear her. "We should probably talk as soon as possible."

Sadness gripped her heart. "I already know, Auntie," Rylie said. Gwyn's eyes widened. "I looked in your room and I saw everything. I'm really sorry. I know I shouldn't have done that."

"Well." She hooked her thumbs in her belt loops and didn't say anything else about it, but Rylie saw her swallow hard. "That's that."

"It's okay. I'm going to stay and help you."

A hint of a smile crossed Gwyn's face. "Are you going to introduce me to your friend?"

Seth walked over and offered her a disarmingly handsome smile. "My name is Seth, ma'am. I'm Abel's brother."

"He mentioned you," she said, and they shook hands. "How long have you and Rylie been... friends?"

"A little while," he said.

"Uh huh." Gwyn gave Rylie a look that said *you have a lot of explaining to do*, but she was polite enough to save it for later. "What are you two doing in the stables?"

"I'm going to ride a horse," Rylie said.

"Really?"

"Really."

Once Butch was ready, Seth and Gwyneth stood back to watch Rylie. The horses were watching her, too. Rylie felt like the whole world was waiting to see what would happen.

All she had to do was mount the horse, but she couldn't make herself move forward. She kept thinking about the last time she reached for a bridle and ended up with a broken collarbone. Even though Butch barely looked awake, Rylie had to hold her breath while she opened his door. He huffed.

"Good horse," she muttered. "I'm not a scary monster. I'm just a girl going for a ride."

He didn't move away when she grabbed the pommel, and he stood still while she climbed on and got her foot in the other stirrup.

Rylie froze on top of him, too afraid to flick the reins.

Gwyn was grinning. "Looking good, babe."

Seth stepped forward to take the bridle. "Hang on, Rylie. We'll do this together."

He led them to the doors, and together, they rode into the daylight.

About the Author

SM Reine is a writer and graphic designer obsessed with werewolves, the occult, and collecting swords. Sara spins tales of dark fantasy to escape the drudgery of the desert, where she lives with her husband, the Helpful Baby, and a small army of black familiars.

Sign up to be notified of new releases!
eepurl.com/eWERY

CPSIA information can be obtained at www.ICGtesting.com
Printed in the USA
LVOW13s1616080814

398214LV00022B/1058/P